Winter's Woman

The Wicked Winters Book Nine

By
Scarlett Scott

Winter's Women
The Wicked Winters Book 9

Published by Happily Ever After Books, LLC
Print Edition

ISBN: 979-8-561740-46-6

Edited by Grace Bradley
Cover Design by Wicked Smart Designs

For more information, contact author Scarlett Scott.
www.scarlettscottauthor.com

The reigning toast of the Season, Lady Evangeline Saltisford is betrothed to the most eligible bachelor in London and a scant few weeks from having everything she has ever wanted. Until danger comes calling, and she is forced to accept aid from a decidedly unlikely—and infuriating—source.

Devil Winter is the illegitimate offspring of a wealthy merchant and a prostitute. He detests fancy aristocrats and has no patience for a cosseted duke's daughter. But he will do anything for his family, and when his older brother asks Devil to play bodyguard to Lady Evie, he has no choice but to accept the loathsome task.

Evie wants nothing to do with the boorish man from the rookeries who favors growls and glowers over polite manners. She is perfectly happy with her handsome, aristocratic fiancé. At least, that is what she tells herself. Until her gruff protector reveals a side she never imagined existed. A side she finds increasingly difficult to resist.

Devil is determined to eliminate the threat to Evie and cull her from his life. But being forced to remain by her side proves not so loathsome a duty after all. And before long, protecting the stunningly gorgeous duke's daughter is only the beginning of what Devil wants to do…

Dedication

For my family and friends, with much love for all your support.

Sin from thy lips? O trespass sweetly urged!
Give me my sin again
- William Shakespeare, ***Romeo and Juliet***

Chapter One

London 1814

HER TWIN SISTER'S mind had turned to pudding.

That was the only reasonable explanation for the words that had just emerged from Lady Adele Winter's mouth.

Lady Evangeline Saltisford stared at her sister, doing her utmost to ignore the hulking monster lurking in the corner of the drawing room.

"You cannot be serious, Addy." Her eyes flicked to the glowering giant.

He was seated in a chair two sizes too small for him, and he looked ridiculous, surrounded by sleekly polished mahogany and all that gilt and silk. His eyes were a piercing shade of blue. Quite like the summer sky. Her stomach did a queer little flip as their gazes met and held. His bold lips tightened to a disapproving slash. She jerked her attention back to her sister, heat rising in her cheeks.

Addy shook her head, her expression mournful. "I am afraid this is no joking matter, Evie. Someone took a shot at you and Lord Denton while you were driving in the park."

"The shot in question likely originated from a pair of drunkards engaged in a duel," Evie dismissed. "It had nothing to do with me."

The beast in the corner of the chamber grumbled something beneath his breath.

Evie cast another glance in his direction. There was something riveting about his face, and she did not like it. More heat curled through her. Her reaction to him was most odd. He could not be more different from her handsome betrothed, Lord Denton, who was golden-haired and slim, with patrician features and elegant hands.

Likely, it was the novelty of such a man. Like Addy's husband Mr. Dominic Winter, the man glaring at her hailed from the rookeries of the East End. Devil Winter was tall, broad, and feral with dark hair worn too long and massive fists, his handsome features set in a perpetual scowl. Everything about him screamed impropriety and the illicit.

And bedchamber romps.

What? No!

She was aghast at herself. Hastily, she dashed the errant thought away.

"Devil is right," Addy was saying, snatching Evie's attention back once more. "We cannot be sure you were not the intended target. Until we know more, you will be safer with him watching over you."

Evie raised a brow. "He said all that? Odd. I could have sworn I heard nothing more than a growl."

Devil Winter grunted.

She ignored him, tamping down the unsettled sensation trying to rise within her. Most unwanted. Unnecessary as well. She was happy with Lord Denton. Soon, she would be his wife. He was everything she had ever wanted in a husband. All she had to do was persuade her well-intentioned sister that having an ill-tempered man torn from the rookeries hanging about would be disastrous for Evie's impeccable reputation.

"Do be nice, Evie," Addy cautioned, frowning at her. "Devil is being quite generous, agreeing to keep you safe."

"Father will have an apoplectic fit when he discovers what you intend to do," she warned her sister in turn.

Their father, the Duke of Linross, had been called away from London to one of his country estates. He had only allowed Evie to remain in London because of her looming nuptials with Lord Denton, a much-needed answer to the scandal Addy had brought to the family with her marriage.

With their mother still in Cornwall and their sister Hannah approaching her lying in, Evie had unceremoniously found herself being chaperoned by her twin sister, who was married to one of London's greatest rogues. The potential scandal was bad enough, but her sister's suggestion a hulking man who went by the name *Devil* ought to offer her protection… Why, it was ludicrous.

"Our father will be grateful I have taken the threat to you seriously and done my sisterly duty." Addy smiled.

"Lord Denton will not like it," she tried next, knowing her betrothed would disapprove most heartily.

Denton adhered to propriety above all else. He had not even attempted to kiss her yet, much to Evie's dismay.

A low growl emanated from the corner of the drawing room, followed by a deep, booming baritone. "Then Denton can go fu—"

"Yes, you are right, Devil," Addy interrupted brightly. "Lord Denton need not know. When you are here at home, Devil will never be far from your side. When you are in public, he will follow you discreetly. Is that not right, Devil?"

He grunted once more.

"No," Evie said mulishly. "I do not *want* him at my side. Nor do I require protection."

"It is necessary, Evie, for your wellbeing." Addy was stern. Insistent.

Evie frowned. "He is menacing, Addy." She lowered her

voice to a whisper. "I do not like him."

"Heard that," he growled. "Feeling's mutual."

Evie's gaze returned to him. Their stares clashed, the connection sending a visceral jolt through her. She could not seem to look away. The certain knowledge that Devil Winter was going to cause her a great deal of trouble lodged in her heart like a thorn.

FUCKING, FUCKING, FUCK.

Why had he agreed to his half brother Dom's bloody asinine request?

Lady Evangeline Saltisford was a golden, saucy bit of baggage. She was the sort of lady who was beautiful and she knew it. The kind who could have any man in London on his knees, ready to lick the soles of her slippers. A duke's daughter. Born to wealth and privilege. One of the quality, she was. The sort of petticoat who would swoon if she ever spied a rat, let alone have to catch one and eat it as her dinner.

She was the sort of woman Devil despised.

And she looked at him now, darting glances of disapproval in his direction every few moments as if he were a rat himself. Speaking about him as if he hadn't a pair of ears to hear or the sawdust betwixt them to understand her speech.

"I do not like him," she told Dom's wife, Lady Adele—her twin—mayhap supposing her dulcet voice could not carry to him.

It could.

"Heard that," he growled. "Feeling's mutual."

For twins, the two of them had not one damned thing in common. Lady Adele was kind and sweet as sugar while her counterpart was lovely as a gem and coldhearted as a lump of coal. Lady Adele's dark-haired loveliness was a distinct contrast to Lady Evangeline's blonde beauty.

Why the devil had he sat in this bleeding chair? It was two sizes too small and pinching his arse.

"I beg your pardon?"

The question broke through his thoughts. Feminine and cutting. As if he had been the one to insult her first.

The quality.

Fuck them all. Except Lady Adele, he added grudgingly. She was not half-bad, and she was in love with his ill-tempered brother, so that was saying something. Dom deserved happiness more than anyone Devil knew.

"You don't like me, my lady," he said, his voice feeling rusty. He did not care much for conversing. "Fine. I don't like you neither."

"Either," she snapped, her eyes locking with his.

His lip curled. "I beg *your* pardon?"

She cleared her throat primly. "The correct manner of speech is to say *I do not like you either*, Mr. Winter. Not *I don't like you neither*. That is most improper form, but do not fear. A hint of correction is good for the constitution, now and then."

He growled. This supercilious chit could go to Hades.

But she did not stop there. One wheaten brow raised. "I am afraid I did not hear your response, sir."

That was because she hadn't gotten one. And if she knew what was good for her, she would stuff her airs up her pretty arse and close her lips. She would not like to hear anything he had to say to her. Likely, it would make her petticoats curl.

"Evie, Devil is doing us all a favor," Lady Adele was telling her sister in quiet reprimand. "We are fortunate indeed. No one can keep you safer than he shall."

This time, the other brow went up, a full show of milady's

disbelief. Someone ought to take her over his knee, throw up her skirts, and spank her. Briefly, he allowed himself the fantasy of imagining her bare bottom, how lush and full it would be, her outrage as his coarse palm connected with her smooth, ivory flesh.

But it wouldn't be Devil. He liked his women soft and seductive and knowing, not tart-tongued and elegant and arrogant.

"He looks as if *he* is the sort of person I ought to be guarded against, Addy. Rather than the opposite."

This judgment, too, was delivered in a whisper. One she undoubtedly believed the simpleton in the corner could not comprehend. Milady was about to receive an education.

He would have risen to his feet had he not feared the goddamn chair would stick to his arse. Instead, he remained where he was, pinning his nemesis with a disparaging stare of his own.

"I *am* the guard, Lady Elizabeth," he snapped, intentionally using the wrong name.

It was small of him, he knew. But enjoyable, nonetheless.

Her shoulders drew back. "My name is Lady Evangeline."

He scowled. "Right. And my name is Devil. Not *Mr. Winter*. Not *sir*. Devil. Repeat it after me if you like."

Her cheeks flushed. "Forgive me, but *Devil* cannot be your Christian name."

Ordinarily, he didn't give a bean when he irritated someone. But there was something about nettling the condescending Lady Evangeline that pleased him. And he hadn't been pleased in…

A long damned time.

"Says who?" he retorted.

She stared at him, aghast.

That was what he thought. Not even a smart retort out of

milady's—

"Says Lady Evangeline Saltisford," she said, her voice dripping with ice. "If I am to suffer this nonsensical guard nonsense, I must insist I cannot refer to you as Devil. It feels far too damning."

Of course it did. That was the point. Enemies tended to think twice about attacking a man named Devil. *Theodore* did not have the same effect. He would eat his cravat before he would tell her his true name.

He shrugged. "Devil or nothing."

"Mr. Nothing is a strange name indeed, but if that is truly what you wish..."

Lady Adele sighed loudly. "Evie, you are behaving abominably."

At last, a voice of reason. That twin sister of hers was right shrewish.

Lady Evangeline's attention returned to her sister. "I am behaving poorly? Heavens, Addy. Ever since you secretly married Mr. Winter, you are acting as if there are goblins hiding behind every corner, waiting to attack us all."

"Suttons *are* goblins," Devil rumbled, surprising himself by speaking again. "Look like them, too."

Two sets of dark eyes flew to him. He ought to have held his sodding tongue. The chair seemed to grow smaller by the minute.

"Who are Suttons?" Lady Evangeline asked, her gaze never wavering from his this time.

She had addressed him. Without a cutting or condescending edge to her tone.

"Enemies of the Winters," he said simply.

Her lips—full and pink and luscious-looking as a berry tart—compressed. "But I am not a Winter."

"Someone shot at you," he pointed out.

The obvious. He still wasn't convinced it had been Suttons, however. Shooting at plump pigeons wasn't their sport. They liked dog and cock fights, chopping off fingers, and setting buildings on fire. The small things.

"No one shot at me! I was on a drive in the park with my betrothed." Her tone rose, veering toward melodrama as she turned back to her sister, addressing her once more. "I deeply regret Lord Denton ever mentioned it, as that single bullet has caused me no end of trouble."

Lord Denton. Devil's lip curled. Of course she would be marrying a soft-palmed twat like Denton who strutted about with a quizzing glass and a cravat tied up to his bloody eyebrows. The bastard had probably shat in his breeches when the shot flew by his curricle.

"He did no such thing!" Lady Evangeline was pinning him with an accusing glare, her face pale. "How dare you, sir? In the presence of ladies…"

Well, fuck.

Had he said that aloud? All of it? Hell of a thing. He had not spoken this much since…

Cora.

Double fuck.

A dark wave of memories hit him in the gut like a fist. It was time to extract himself from this cursed chair and go. He would find his brother and tell Dom this particular assignment was not for him. Loyalty and brotherly devotion had a limit. This was it. Lady Evangeline Saltisford could take her airs and her golden beauty and marry her silly fop and have his heir and spare and then cry into her embroidered handkerchief when she discovered he had a mistress.

He stood, narrowly hauling himself from betwixt the polished arms of the mahogany chair of death, and bowed. Devil knew he ought to say something. Likely an apology. But in the end, he couldn't be bothered. He stalked from the drawing room with Lady Evangeline Saltisford's indignation trailing after him.

Along with her scent.

She smelled like a damned fruit, sweet and ripe.

Curse her.

Chapter Two

"I KNOW YOU are hopelessly in love with your husband, Addy, but this farce cannot continue."

Evie paused in practicing the delivery of her speech to the cheval glass in her chamber, studying her reflection. Did she look angry? That would never do. She knew her twin. Addy did not like strife. Evie would need to be calm. Cool. Soft, even.

She took a deep breath and then made another attempt.

"After the improper manner in which he referred to Lord Denton yesterday, you cannot possibly expect me to suffer Mr. Winter's presence."

No.

That would not do either. Addy was quite protective of her new husband's family. Because her sister possessed a heart of gold, it did not matter to Addy that the branch of the Winter family she had married into was scandalous. That their accents and lack of proper manners gave their upbringing in the rookery away. No, indeed. She believed it an excellent idea to bring more of them to Mayfair.

One great, surly beast in particular.

Devil Winter.

Nay, Evie refused to think of him as such. Instead, she would think of him as *Mr. Nothing*. And one could only hope that soon enough he *would* be nothing in her life, returned to the gaming hell where he belonged, along with his disturbingly blue eyes and the wickedest lips she had ever seen upon a man.

Why did he have to be so…

Oh, bother. She would not think it.

Another slow, deep breath, and she tried again.

"I know you are only concerned for me, my dearest sister. However, I am certain the shot that was fired in the park was not meant—"

Her words died.

Because in the next moment, the world exploded. Everything seemed to happen, all at once.

A loud report was followed by the shattering of glass. The window of her chamber fell to the floor in a thousand pieces. Something whisked past her shoulder, leaving a stinging sensation in its wake. Bits of plaster ceiling and dust rained down from overhead.

Her arm was wet. Wet and burning. Tickling. Something was sticky and warm on her flesh. She pressed a hand to the sleeve of her gown, her fingers finding it torn and ragged. More wetness greeted her fingertips.

In shock, she examined her fingers.

They were dripping with scarlet.

Blood. Her own.

Dear God, she had been shot.

A scream tore from her throat.

Her vision turned dark around the edges. She felt hot, then cold. The prickle of perspiration broke out on her forehead. And then her knees went weak. The door to her chamber burst open, and the faint sound of a deep voice calling her name reached her.

But it was too late.

Her world went black.

DEVIL WAS ACCUSTOMED to all manner of violence. Knife attacks, gunshot wounds, fires. The only constant in the rookeries was that anything could happen at any time, and a man was never truly safe. He was always prepared, even in his sleep.

But the gunshots fired into his half brother's Mayfair townhome?

He had not been expecting them.

Dom and Lady Adele were not at home this morning, having both gone to The Devil's Spawn, leaving Devil to the work of beginning his new plan of protecting the townhome and its occupants. One moment, he was instructing his men on where they were to be stationed, and the next, the unmistakable sound of shots being fired erupted from the street. He was running before the shattering glass and the scream. Heart thundering in his chest, he plowed through the door of Lady Evangeline's chamber.

One of the windows was shattered, shards glittering all over the floor as the window dressings blew in the wind. She was on the floor in a heap of cream-colored skirts and crimson blood.

Devil was on his knees at her side in an instant. The sleeve of her gown was torn, covered in red. Her fingers were coated, her face pale. But her breathing was steady, her bosom rising and falling. He wasted no time in lifting her in his arms and carrying her from the chamber, lest there was any further danger. Such a tiny thing she was, light as a bird in his arms. She felt like something fragile and delicate, fashioned of porcelain rather than human flesh. But she was all too real, capable of being harmed. Her blood spilled.

Fuck.

He needed to assess the extent of her wounds.

His men caught up to him in the hall.

"Get to the street," he barked at them as he carried a limp Lady Evangeline toward his chamber. "Find the bastard responsible for this!"

They hurried to do his bidding. He stalked down the hall to the guest chamber he had been given and shouldered his way through the door. Lady Evangeline was coming to in his arms, groaning. He laid her on his bed, taking care not to jostle her.

Golden lashes fluttered. Gently, he brushed the curls framing her face aside. Her eyes opened, wide, brown pools. The color was returning to her cheeks. All good signs.

"Where are you injured?" he asked, assessing her bleeding wound.

Through the ruined fabric, he detected what appeared to be a long line on her upper arm.

"Just…my arm. I think." She blinked, then struggled to sit up.

He kept her still by flattening his palm over her unwounded shoulder. "No moving."

He needed to make certain she was not bleeding anywhere else. It was possible a lone bullet had grazed her and that was the extent of the damage. But he had also seen men with bullets lodged in their backs who had been in shock and hadn't realized they had been wounded.

Devil tore off the remainder of her sleeve and pressed it lightly to her wound, staying the blood flow. She inhaled sharply, her body tensing at the pain. Anger sliced through him. Someone had dared to shoot through the window of Dom's home in the midst of fancy Mayfair. And Lady Evangeline had been injured. Someone intended to do her harm. And Devil had failed to protect her.

"Do you have pain anywhere else?" he asked her, his voice more gruff than he intended.

He was bloody furious. Furious at the unknown enemy who had hurt her, furious at himself for not preventing it from happening.

"No." She shifted again, trying to sit up.

Once more, he flattened his hand against her collarbone, preventing her from moving. "Stay still. I need to make certain you aren't hurt anywhere else."

"Where did you bring me?" she demanded, some of her queenly ice returning. "I cannot be alone with you in a bedchamber, Mr. Winter."

Milady was back.

He released his pressure on her wound and made a cursory search of her person, ignoring her outrage. She'd been shot, damn it.

"What are you doing, sir?" she asked as he flipped up her skirts.

He had a brief glimpse at the paradise beneath her petticoats. Petite legs encased in stockings, curved thighs.

No wounds, so he settled her gown back into place. "Checking you for signs of injury."

"I told you my only wound is my arm." She wriggled, as if trying to escape him.

But he possessed more strength in his pinky finger than she did in her entire body. Keeping her where he wanted her proved no challenge. "Stop talking."

"You are incredibly rude, sir!"

He ignored her, making quick work of checking her everywhere he could before returning his attention to her sole wound. She had been fortunate. If the bullet had lodged within her arm…

No, he would not think of that now.

The bleeding had already slowed, but there was the possibility she would need to be stitched up. His half sister Genevieve was a wonder with the needle. The wound would also require cleaning. He wondered if Dom had any whisky in this wealthy nib house of his.

"Stay here," he ordered her. "Wait for me."

Then he stalked off in search of supplies, aid, and answers.

HE HAD ISSUED his command to her as if she were a dog.

Even in pain, her wounded arm throbbing, Evie had no intention of doing Devil Winter's bidding. He could go back to Hades where he belonged. Besides, was he not meant to be guarding her? And yet, during his supposed watch, someone had fired a bullet through her window.

And she was bleeding. Wounded. Part of her still felt as if it had all been a nightmare, and that any moment she would wake to find herself beneath the counterpane. But the pain radiating from her arm reminded her the predicament in which she found herself helplessly mired was all too real. As did her surroundings.

The arrogant oaf had carried her to a guest chamber she suspected was his.

Which meant…she was on his bed. The bed where he had slept last night. And his hands had been on her. He had looked beneath her gown and petticoats. He had taken shocking liberties with her person.

Lord Denton would not be pleased if he discovered, she had no doubt.

Evie slid from the bed, clutching her torn sleeve to the wound lest she bleed everywhere. The blood on her hand, already drying, made her feel as if her head were too light for her body. It also made the room swirl a bit around the edges as she swayed toward the door.

She had scarcely made it to the threshold when a loud growl, accompanied by the thud of large footsteps, told her that her unwanted bodyguard had returned.

"Damn it, I told you to wait."

She was in his arms again, unceremoniously hauled sideways, the world upended. He carried her with ease, ignoring her protests as he placed her back on the bed, moving slowly to avoid jostling her wounded arm.

The care he showed her seemed quite at odds with the gruffness of his nature. So, too, the angry growl. Mayhap it was the dizziness still assailing her, or the loss of blood. But she found herself studying him. He was more handsome at this proximity than she had supposed. The concentration on his countenance heightened the sharp prominence of his cheekbones and jaw. He caught his lower lip between his teeth as he took her wrist in a tender grasp and removed her hand from the wound.

"You are not a doctor," she told him. "I will wait for the family physician to examine me."

In typical Devil Winter fashion, he ignored her. Using a cloth, he dabbed gently at her wound, mopping up the blood. Her breath caught at the pain his small action sent roiling through her.

"That hurt!" she accused, though in truth she knew he was doing his utmost to avoid causing her further discomfort.

He reached for a bottle of spirits he must have fetched during his brief disappearance. Slowly, he slid an arm behind her back, helping her to lift her head from the pillow. Then, he held the bottle to her lips.

"Drink."

She hadn't time to protest, and anything she may have

said was drowned beneath a tide of burning liquid as he tipped the bottle and poured some of its contents into her mouth. Whatever it was, it tasted wretched. The urge to spit it everywhere rose, along with a gag. As if sensing her reaction, he pinched her nose. The action had her swallowing instinctively so she could inhale through her burning lips and tongue. Her eyes watered.

"What are you doing?" With her good arm, she attempted to push him away from her.

But the effort was no use. It was akin to an ant attempting to shift a boulder. Devil Winter was not going anywhere.

Instead of answering her, he put the bottle to her mouth once more. "Drink again."

"No." Even as she spoke the word, he slid the bottle between her lips and tilted it.

Another rush of burning, terribly dry liquid hit her tongue. This time, she swallowed it down without his prompting, for what choice had she? An oaken flavor remained, bitter. But a strange warmth blossomed within Evie. Some of the panic bristling inside her faded.

He allowed her to swallow before tipping the bottle. More went down her throat. A drop of it slipped from the corner of her lips and slid down her face. He caught it with his thumb before she could react, the rough graze of the callused pad on her skin strangely intimate.

Their gazes met and held. Such brilliant, beautiful blue. His lashes were long and thick, she noted. The architecture of his face was a strange blend of wildness and perfection, of sinner and savior. The pain in her arm reminded her what had happened, where she was, and with whom.

She blinked. "I do not want any more of that poison."

"Not poison." He held it to her mouth once more. "Whisky. Drink, Lady Evangeline. It will ease the stinging."

She took another drag of the spirits as he requested. This would have her bosky in no time.

Evangeline eyed him, the patience in his countenance, the impassiveness of his expression. "Have you ever been shot, sir?"

"Thrice." The bottle was back at her lips.

Was it her imagination, or had his hand crept to her nape? Were those his fingers massaging her neck, easing the stiffness from her muscles? Surely she was delusional.

Belatedly, it occurred to her he had admitted to having been shot.

On no less than three occasions.

She ought not to be surprised, and yet the knowledge he had been in a similar position in his past startled her. "Who shot you?"

"My enemies. One more sip, milady."

She obliged, because his whisky was doing things to her. Softening her. Warming her. Blurring her pain, making it smooth around the edges. Not so hard and furious. He was helping her. Something in his fierce demeanor had shifted.

Or mayhap something inside her had.

Blood loss, she thought for the second time.

Perhaps she was on her deathbed, for there was no other reason to be entertaining the utterly outlandish thought that Mr. Devil Winter was not every bit as barbaric, vulgar, and horrible as she had initially supposed him to be.

"How are you feeling?" he asked.

As if a torpor had settled over her.

"Better," she allowed.

"Good." He tipped the bottle, splashing enough of it on a fresh cloth to dampen it, and then he pressed that cloth to her wound.

The pain was almost unbearable. Every speck of goodwill

toward him instilled by the whisky died a swift death. She screamed and attempted to swat him away with her good hand. But her actions were as futile as before. Devil Winter was a strong, massive man. Immovable.

His face was a study in determination as he went about his task, dashing more whisky on the bloodied cloth before using it to wipe her wound once more. She tried to box his ear but he caught her wrist and held her still as he finished cleaning her bloodied arm.

"You are hurting me," she gritted through her clenched jaws and a haze of tears.

"I am helping you."

It hardly seemed so from her perspective.

"You are punishing me," she countered. "You do not like me. Your disdain for me was evident yesterday."

His full lips quirked, but he did not remove his gaze from her wounded arm. "Disdain. Fancy word for a fancy duke's daughter. Not so fancy when you're shot, are you?"

"Not so excellent a guard when the woman you are tasked with protecting is wounded, are you?" The bitter accusation left her before she could think better of it.

He did not say a word, and if her taunt had upset him, there was no sign of it. Not a hesitation or a tightening of his lips. Why was she staring at his mouth? She had never in her life consumed whisky until this evening. Being soused and shot, after having suffered a loss of blood, was having an ill effect upon her mind.

Instead, he worked in silence, finishing cleaning her wound before taking up a small pot and unscrewing the lid.

"What is that?" she demanded.

"Horse piss."

She blinked at him. Surely she had misheard?

"Rat shit," he said, and then stabbed two of his cloth-covered fingers into the jar, pulling up a generous glob of thick, amber-colored syrup.

He was not serious, was he? He was saying something horrible, was he not? The delusions were settling in now, surely. She felt faint.

He slathered the solution on her wound with slow, gentle motions. "May not need to be stitched up after all."

The burning pain eased. In its place, coolness and a strange sense of numbness settled in. She watched him as he worked, his expression intense. The pain seemed to ease with each brush of the thick ointment. The scent of it filled the air between them. Sweet and herbal.

"Honey?" she asked.

"Amongst other herbs." He finished his work and began winding a length of clean cloth around her arm in a loose grasp. "You may call for your physician as you like, my lady, but I do not think you will need any stitches on this wound. If you are fortunate, it will not fester."

Everything inside her felt brittle and bright. His face was too handsome. His fingers scraping over her tender flesh as he bound her wound too intimate, too warm.

"Horse piss," she said, repeating what he had told her. "And rat shit? Mixed together?"

His gaze jerked to hers. Bluer than the sky and the ocean combined. "Pardon?"

Had he already forgotten his crude words? She was experiencing a curious combination of pain, spirits, and shock. The aftereffects left her feeling as if she were afloat in an ascension balloon. High above and giddy.

"The salve you applied to my wound," she clarified, playing his game. "Is it horse piss mixed with rat shit? Or were you deceiving me, Mr. Nothing?"

He blinked. The corners of his too-full lips twitched.

Almost as if he was tempted to smile. Evie did not think she had ever seen a true smile from Devil Winter yet. A challenge, that. The urge to cause one rose within her, warring with everything else.

"Mr. Nothing?" he repeated, tying off the bandage on her arm with easy, facile motions.

His fingers were long.

His hands were tremendous, just as large as the rest of him.

She found herself strangely entranced with them.

"Devil or nothing," she reminded him. "That is what you said. Therefore, Mr. Nothing it is."

A dark brow quirked. "Is that so, my lady?"

"Evie," she said, and she did not know why.

A second brow joined the first. Such an exquisite display of emotion from his often-stark face. She was most pleased with herself for having caused it.

"Evie," he repeated in his low baritone.

The voice that rumbled down her spine like a forbidden caress.

"Yes." She was feeling deliciously warm and dizzy once again. "More whisky, if you please?"

"I reckon you have had enough." He swallowed, his gaze dipping to her lips.

Or had she imagined it?

"One more sip." Her tone was wheedling, she knew. The stuff tasted awful, but it had knocked the edge off her pain. Or mayhap that was his honey-and-herb concoction.

He stared at her, that impossibly blue gaze seeming to cut straight through her. An indeterminate span of time passed. She was certain he was going to deny her.

And then, he made a sound low in his throat. More of a grunt than anything, and he held the bottle to her lips once more. She took another long draught and thought that perhaps Devil Winter was not quite as horrible as she initially supposed.

Chapter Three

"No."

"Absolutely not."

Devil's lone, low denial rang out at the same time Lady Evangeline's did.

Evie.

Damn it, why did her tap-hackled command he call her by her diminutive return to haunt him now? Didn't matter. All that *did* was his canceling the poorly conceived, half-arsed, utterly shite idea which had just been presented by Lady Adele and Dom. A half brother ought to have more loyalty, the bastard.

"I know it is unusual for a young lady to suddenly be forced to take time away from the social whirl in the midst of the Season," Lady Adele began tentatively, addressing her twin. "However, the events of two days ago leave us with little choice. Surely you must see the necessity of keeping your whereabouts hidden until we can be assured of your safety."

"I most certainly do not." Milady was at her best once more, sweeping through the drawing room as if she were a queen attended by her mere vassals.

Trifling matters such as gunshot wounds did precious little to dampen her aristocratic airs. Devil suspected they were bred in her. She was a duke's daughter, was she not? She had probably emerged from the womb looking down her nose at everyone who was not a lord or lady.

Whilst he had been born fighting for his existence. The woman who had birthed Devil—he refused to think of her as his mother—had not given a bloody bean about him. After he reached a suitable age, selling him had proven a better prospect than attempting to feed an extra mouth had. And Anne Smythe had done just that, may she rot.

"Lady Evangeline, you are in grave danger," his half brother Dom was saying now. "You were fortunate your injuries were not worse. Until we know who is behind these attacks, I am afraid there is no other way of keeping you safe."

There were other ways, damn it.

Devil was certain.

He scowled at Dom. "I don't go to the monkery. London is where I stay."

He had made this clear when he had first been approached with this Bedlamite's plan of secreting Lady Evangeline to the countryside with Devil as her squire. He did not like the country. Bricks, rats, and streets that stunk of desperation suited him fine. He knew what to expect here. Knew how to fight and protect himself.

The East End was his territory. This Mayfair business was a lot of donkey dung, but he had been willing to suffer it temporarily out of loyalty to Dom. Not the country, however. Not traveling with milady.

Not in this fucking century.

"London is where you have stayed, but there is no reason you cannot remove yourself from it for a time," Dom was telling him in his calm, persuasive, I-can-make-you-do-as-I-wish, older-brother tone. "I traveled to Oxfordshire, if you will recall, and I returned whole."

"Married." Devil's lip curled of its own accord.

He liked his brother's wife, it was true. However, there

was no denying that his brother's trip to the monkery had landed him leg-shackled. As planned, yes. But thoroughly besotted with his wife.

Terrible state. Horrible example to offer.

Devil wanted no part of marriage. He had fancied himself in love once. But Cora's defection had robbed him of any capacity to feel. He was invulnerable now. Cold as ice, hard as a wall.

"He returned married to me," Lady Adele reminded Devil gently. "I do not think it such a horrid fate. There is nothing wrong with marriage, Devil. But it is not as if you need fear such a circumstance befalling you. Evie is betrothed to Lord Denton."

Ah, yes, he thought acidly. How could he have forgotten? Not that a fine lady such as Lady Evie would ever deign to consider an East End criminal such as himself a prospect. She would never have allowed him to touch her after her wounding, had she not been incapacitated and in her cups. He was not fit to kiss milady's soiled hem.

If indeed milady's hems were ever soiled. He rather doubted it.

"That is why I must not leave London," Evie countered, her voice triumphant.

She was dressed in a pale-pink gown, the bandage on her upper arm cleverly disguised by her sleeve. One would never guess anything ill had befallen her. Lady Evangeline Saltisford was the epitome of elegance and perfection. Even her golden curls were neat little screws framing her lovely face, nary a one out of place.

"Your betrothal to Lord Denton?" Lady Adele asked her sister. "You are not going to be married for another three months, dearest. We are only suggesting you remove yourself for a fortnight. Perhaps less."

A fortnight with milady?

Christ no.

Devil suppressed a shudder.

"If I am to suddenly disappear for a fortnight, it will be remarked upon," Lady Evie countered. "Widely. How do you propose I am to explain it?"

"There will be no explanation," Devil bit out. "Because I ain't squiring you anywhere. I don't leave London."

Dom sighed. "I was afraid you would prove unyielding on that. Fair enough. If you do not want to go to the country, Devereaux has offered the use of one of his townhomes."

Wrong person to mention.

"Devereaux, is it?" he growled, nettled to hear Dom speak of their legitimate half brother as if they were now on friendly terms.

To say nothing of the grandiosity of such a gesture. *Townhomes*, Dom had said, as if there were more than one.

How many townhomes did one arsehole need?

Dom raked a hand through his hair, his jaw hardening with annoyance. "I am persuaded our half brother is not who I once thought him to be. He has proven himself. Need I remind you of the manner in which he aided us with the Suttons and their waterworks?"

Yes, Devereaux Winter had indeed facilitated the deal with the Suttons. The Sutton Waterworks belonged to the Winters now. But Devil did not trust any man as far as he could throw him. And Deveraux Winter was a massive man. Devil did not suppose he could throw him farther than a puddle's length.

Devil snorted. "And who is taking shots at Lady Evangeline? You do not suppose it is Suttons?"

"I cannot be sure." Dom shook his head. "I cannot believe they would be foolish enough to upset the balance so soon after calling a truce. I need time to dig into this without worrying over Lady Evie's wellbeing. Be reasonable, Devil."

He did not feel like being reasonable. *Reasonable* was for nibs who worried about the knot in their cravats and the shine on their boots.

Devil shook his head. "A fortnight is impossible."

"I agree wholeheartedly," Lady Evangeline said. "It is impossible. You cannot expect me to hide myself somewhere with…Mr. Devil. Lord Denton shall never forgive me if I am to disappear. I am promised to attend the Farthington ball tomorrow, and the Desmond musicale the day after. My absence will be noted."

"Your absence is necessary for your protection," Lady Adele said.

She had a point, and Devil hated to admit it. Indeed, he *would* admit it if anyone other than himself was being cozened into playing her guard for the next fortnight. Bad enough to remain in milady's presence when he had Dom to speak to. Unless…

"The two of you would accompany us," Devil said.

"No." Dom passed a hand over his jaw. "I need to remain here, to run The Devil's Spawn, and to determine who is behind these attacks and why."

"Why not me?" Devil suggested. "I remain. You and Lady Adele take Lady Evangeline to the countryside or to Winter's townhome. I will stay and watch over The Devil's Spawn and find the bastard responsible for shooting Lady Evangeline."

Sound plan, as far as Devil was concerned. No more milady. No more golden curls and taunting berry lips. No more unwanted cockstands in her presence.

Dom sighed. "It cannot be me. You know as well as I do what happened the last time I distanced myself from London. There were fires set at our hell, men attempting to ruin us."

On Devil's watch.

His brother did not need to say it. Devil had inwardly lashed himself a thousand times for his failure to lead the ship in Dom's absence. The Devil's Spawn had not been reduced to ashes. But the damage had been bad enough.

Guilt and disappointment at his own failures sliced through him. Dom was right to distrust him. Not only had Devil been unable to keep the hell safe; Lady Evie had been shot on his second day acting as guard.

Fuck.

He owed his brother. And he owed it to himself to do better this time. To prove his mettle. Even if it meant keeping milady company for two weeks in Devereaux Winter's house.

Damn.

Hell.

Devil nodded once, his gaze never straying from Dom's. "Fair enough. I owe you. I'll do what I must."

Dom nodded. "Thank you, brother."

He bowed and fled the fancy drawing room—dripping in gilt and polished mahogany—as Lady Evangeline sent up a fresh round of protests.

EVIE WANTED TO kick something.

Or shout.

Pound her fist into a wall? No, that would hurt.

She wanted to snatch up something dear and hurl it to the floor, watching as it shattered into myriad pieces. Irreparable.

Just as her reputation would be by the time this farce had come to an end. They may as well find the villain who had been attempting to murder her and have him shoot her now.

"Sixteen."

The mocking voice of Devil Winter reached her then. A rough, growling rumble. Why had he spoken? She was doing her utmost to pretend he was not standing in the corner of this unfamiliar library, watching her pace.

The library was large.

The book selection was excellent.

Under ordinary circumstances, she would have been well-pleased. But this was decidedly *not* ordinary circumstances. This was, instead, Bedlamite, ridiculous, untenable, unacceptable circumstances. And she was furious.

Ignoring the massive oaf in the room, she spun on her slipper-clad heel and stalked back down the Aubusson.

"Seventeen."

His voice was amused. The low, intimate tone of it trilled down her spine. Made her belly tighten and her skin feel flushed. Was that his scent on the air? Spice and bay and leather?

Curse the man.

Mayhap if she ignored him, he would go away. His presence in this chamber was not just unwanted but bewilderingly improper. Her lady's maid, who was to act as chaperone, was upstairs, seeing to the unpacking of Evie's trunks. The lumbering brute who watched her now was supposed to be elsewhere.

Not plaguing her with his handsome presence.

Handsome? For shame, Evie. What would Lord Denton say?

She shook that unsettling question from her mind. Lord Denton had been sent a letter, carefully written by Evie herself before she had been surreptitiously swept from her sister and brother-in-law's townhome. Five carriages had set off at once lest any unseen foes had been watching and anticipating their movement. And Evie had been inside the only one which had also contained *him*.

"Eighteen."

His mocking voice reached her once more.

She halted in her pacing and turned toward him, irritation surpassing all else. "Shall I applaud you, Mr. Nothing? You can count. I am astounded a man of your background is capable of such a rudimentary skill."

If her tone was biting, and if her words were horrid, it could hardly be helped. She was feeling unsettled, terrified, and cruel, all at once.

Devil Winter remained stoic, his expression never shifting from sardonic amusement. His face was, as ever, a source of astonishment. He was the sort of gentleman one looked upon with an involuntary inhalation of breath at the power of his rugged, masculine beauty.

However, upon closer inspection, she detected a subtle change in his bearing. A stiffening of his posture. Her words had hit their mark, though he was doing his utmost to feign indifference. The realization gave Evie no joy. Instead, shame swamped her. He said nothing, simply watched her, impassive.

This new silence somehow mocked her more than his counting had. She was furious with him for capitulating and agreeing to this madcap scheme of Adele and Mr. Winter's. Being trapped inside a strange house with no one for company save servants and Devil Winter was akin to torture.

How was she to bear a fortnight of this?

"Well?" she demanded, aware that she was being cutting and rude to him and yet somehow unable to stop herself. "Have you anything to say now, Mr. Nothing?"

She had been shot. She had been torn from the life to which she was accustomed. She had been forced to lie to her future husband. She had been hidden away. How could anyone expect her to be anything other than bitter and upset and ill-mannered? She was sure they could not, Devil Winter included.

"Devil."

That was what the man had to say. The curt, nonsensical insistence she refer to him as his awful sobriquet. She most certainly would not.

Evie spun on her heel and commenced pacing.

"Nineteen."

She turned back to him. "You are counting the number of times I have paced the floor?"

He stared at her with those insolent blue eyes that saw too much and made her tingle in places she had not previously known existed. He said nothing.

Somehow, his silence was a greater rebuke than his words.

"You refuse to answer me until I refer to you as you wish" she guessed next, irritated. "I do not want to play games with you, sir."

He grunted.

She gritted her teeth, commencing her pacing.

"Twenty."

That was it.

She pivoted and stalked toward him. Evie did not halt until she was near enough to thrust out her forefinger and poke him in his big, hard chest. "Stop. Counting."

Two pokes, one for each word. Emphasizing her point.

He raised a brow and said nothing, mocking her without uttering a syllable.

Her finger lingered against his chest, and it occurred to her belatedly that he had somehow shucked his coat. He stood before her in shirtsleeves and a waistcoat only, the cravat at his neck scarcely knotted. In a word, he looked disreputable.

And delicious.

No! Decidedly not that.

She banished the unworthy thought immediately. The warmth emanating from him seared her fingertip. She cleared her throat. Forgot why she was still touching him. His scent was richer at this proximity, tiny flecks of green visible in his bright eyes. Her gaze dipped to his mouth, which was full.

Fuller than Lord Denton's. She did not think she could recall her betrothed's lips just now. *Oh, bother.*

"Like what you see, milady?"

His mocking query filled her with mortification. Her cheeks were scalding. She withdrew her finger. "No. I am horrified by it. You are a dreadful, uncouth beast, sir."

One corner of his lips quirked. "Didn't seem horrified."

She was staring at his dratted mouth again. And being insolent. He had cleaned her wound when she had been injured. His balm had appeared to stave off infection and was aiding in her healing. She had not required stitching after all, much to her relief.

But Evie was still in a dreadful mood. Her life had been disrupted. Upended. Her reputation was in every bit as much danger as her life. If word of her sojourn in this Grosvenor Square townhome ever reached anyone, she would never survive the storm of scandal. Diamonds of the first water did not disappear for a fortnight with the sole accompaniment of a lady's maid and one of the East End's most feared criminals.

"Milady?" he prompted, his voice still mocking.

What was it about him? Why could she not seem to look away, to walk away?

She sniffed. "As a lady, one must hide one's true feelings. Undoubtedly, that is why I do not seem horrified by you. However, rest assured that I am."

The other corner of his mouth lifted. "If you say so, milady."

His scent was coiling around her now. Much as she imagined a serpent would. She had to put some distance between them. "No more counting, Mr. Nothing."

Once more, he declined to respond, simply watching her with that mocking smile on his sensual lips.

On a huff, Evie turned and resumed her pacing.

"One-and-twenty."

She whirled back to him. "I did not finish my twentieth pace. How can we now be at one-and-twenty?"

He cocked his head. "Devil."

"What is your true Christian name? No mother would name her child Devil."

"You do not know the woman who birthed me."

That was a decidedly strange manner to refer to one's mother, she thought. His jaw had tightened. A sensitive subject, she sensed. *Hmm. Interesting.* His intellect and his mother. Twin weaknesses from the monster of a man who was to haunt her every day. She would save the knowledge, lest she needed it.

"I wish to read," she announced, deciding a change of subject was in order. "There is no need for you to remain here."

"I stay where you are."

She glared. "You cannot be where I am at every hour of the day."

"When I was not, you were shot."

"No one knows I am here."

He shrugged. "We hope."

Her stomach felt as if it dropped to the floor. "What was the meaning of the five carriages, if not to confuse anyone who could be watching?"

"It is early to tell if we were followed. I saw no sign of it, but nothing in life is certain."

Evie frowned. "That is a grim view of the world, sir."

"A truthful view." Another shrug of those impossibly broad shoulders.

Her gaze dipped to his chest. To his throat. To his jaw, shadowed with a fine layer of whiskers. Back to his lips. She wondered for the first time why he was so quiet, so solemn, so jaded. What had happened to Devil Winter in his past to make him the man he was?

Then she wondered why she cared.

Most certainly, she should not. Thinking of him at all was dangerous. As was lingering near to him. And yet she did.

They stared at each other, at an impasse.

"I do not wish to be here," she said.

He raised an inky brow, saying nothing.

Fair enough. He had made his opinion on the matter clear as well. Some of her irritation with him faded. He was not the source of her ire. Indeed, mayhap he was every bit as trapped as she was.

"You have more of a choice than I do," she countered, as if he had spoken aloud.

Sky-blue eyes burned into hers, unwavering. "You do not know my brother."

"Nonsense. Gentlemen possess all the power. A man can be anything he wishes, go anywhere as he pleases. A lady, meanwhile, is held to the strictest of standards."

"Not in the rookeries."

His world was different from hers. The reminder nettled more than it should. She was suddenly acutely aware of her own life as the daughter of a duke. She had been raised without thought of anyone who had less.

"What is it like there?" she ventured, curious in spite of herself.

He grunted.

Apparently, she had reached the limit of his goodwill.

Either that, or Devil Winter did not like to speak of his past.

"I am going to read," she announced. "You may as well. Take your pick. There is no end of books here."

He said nothing, merely watched her.

On an irritated sigh, she turned away from him once more.

"Twenty."

This time, she carried on, stalking to the wall of books opposite her. The man was maddening. Vexing. Infuriating. She was not sure if she ought to be amused at his return to twenty in his counting of her pacing or incensed. Evie settled for somewhere in between the two as she searched the endless spines before her, looking for a book to suitably distract and entertain. He had not joined her, of course.

But she felt his eyes upon her back, burning into her, watching.

Her finger drifted over a volume of Shakespeare just as an unsettling conclusion occurred to her. Two subjects had pierced Devil Winter's armor. His intellect and his mother. He could count, but was it possible he could not read? She had no notion of what the education of a young man in the rookeries would be. Her sister's husband could read, but that did not necessarily mean Devil could. They had not shared the same mother, after all.

She plucked *Romeo and Juliet* from the shelf and turned back to him. "Do you mind if I read aloud?"

For a lengthy pause, he said nothing. Merely held her stare. Just when she thought he would not answer, he tipped up his chin. "If you wish, milady."

She settled herself upon a divan, obliging him to fold his tall body into a nearby chair that was, as the chairs at her sister's townhome, comically little for a man of his size.

"That chair is far too small for you," she pointed out.

He growled.

She sighed. "Come and sit here on the settee with me, if you please. You look like a giant sitting in a dollhouse chair."

A grumble emerged from him.

She waited. "I will not begin reading until you move."

Why was she being so persistent? It was not as if she truly wanted him near.

Was it?

Of course not. She was merely trying to be polite. To make amends for her surliness earlier.

They stared at each other. Finally, he sighed and rose, stalking across the Aubusson before settling himself upon the settee at her side. Though the settee was large, Devil Winter was larger still. He crowded her with his big body and his nearness, his scent wafting over her, curling around her. Taunting. His heat radiating.

She swallowed, flipped open the book, and began reading to distract herself. "'Two houses, both alike in dignity'..."

Chapter Four

THE DAYS HAD begun to pass, and blessedly without incident. No more gunshots. His men keeping watch on the perimeter reported nary a sign of anything suspicious. Nothing of greater concern than a stray cat trying to get mounted and a drunkard in the mews, attempting to take a piss. The cat and the man had been chased away with ease.

For the third evening in a row, Devil awaited Lady Evie in the library. Their secret life at Devereaux Winter's spare townhome in Grosvenor Square had settled into an almost eerie ease.

As she had each night following dinner—he took his with the servants while she enjoyed her meal in the dining room as was proper—Lady Evie swept over the threshold. Her gown this evening was almost ethereal, her wild, golden hair scarcely confined. Curls had sprung forth to frame her lovely face.

For the first time since their odd little evening routine had begun, she smiled at the sight of him. A welcoming, bright smile. The sort of smile a man could not help but to feel in his prick.

Fuck. He was not meant to feel an inkling of attraction for Lady Evangeline Saltisford, aristocrat, sister-in-law to his brother. She had a betrothed. Lord Denton, he reminded himself, and not without an accompanying surge of bitterness.

Where the hell was that emerging from?

He tamped down all his emotions—unwanted as they were—for he was excellent at feeling nothing. At hiding everything. He was a wall when he chose to be. Impassive. Imperceptible. Rigid. He'd had to be so for years now.

"More *Romeo and Juliet*?" she asked cheerfully, as if she were happy to see him there, waiting for her like a puppy longing for a pat on the head.

Christ. How pathetic, Devil Winter lingering in the library for a lady to come and read some drivel to him. He wondered if she had guessed he could not read. If this was her attempt at a truce between them. Or perhaps pity, if she suspected the truth.

At times, over the years, he had wished to change his inability to comprehend the written word. Nothing had done him a whit of good. His brother Dom read with ease. He had learned on his own. But Devil's mind was different. The woman who had birthed him had called him a stupid little twat and boxed his ears regularly.

Mayhap he *was* stupid. He got on well enough. He could count. He could tally ledgers. But words eluded him. He could make his mark. *Theodore Winter* was all he could manage. The letters seemed scrambled every time he made an attempt at making sense of words. And so he had made more sense of other things, finding his worth in his strength and his fearlessness and his cunning.

Until now.

When Lady Evie Saltisford read to him, he had realized for the first time what he had been missing. To be sure, her soft, husky voice enhanced the pleasure. But it was also the words coming alive, the characters, the scenes, that took his mind to a new place. A previously unoccupied place.

He was enjoying listening to her read.

Much to his shame.

Devil Winter did not enjoy such nonsense. Or at least, he had not.

"Mr. Winter?" she pressed. "Shall I read more tonight?"

He ought to tell her no. She had been referring to him as Mr. Winter since they had begun this nightly ritual. Better than Mr. Nothing, he supposed. But sitting on the settee by her side was a form of torture.

He cleared his throat. "If it pleases you, milady."

"It pleases me greatly." A warm, sweet smile curved her lips. "Otherwise, I am dreadfully bored, trapped in this place."

She crossed the carpets. Devil tried not to watch the way she glided, with such elegant ease. Or the way the drapery of her gown clung to her hips. Or the creamy expanse of her bosom on display. His cock was standing at attention, and he was imagining what color her nipples would be.

Hellfire and damnation.

He forced himself to move, folding his too-large frame into a fancy chair that scarcely contained him. It was deuced uncomfortable and it killed his ardor whilst putting some necessary distance between himself and Lady Evie.

She pulled the ribbon she had been using to mark her page from the volume and glanced up at him, a frown marring her forehead. It was the most displeased expression she had directed toward him since the day of their arrival.

Interesting.

"Why are you sitting over there, Mr. Winter?"

Her query and curious stare were as unwanted as the unexpected attraction he felt to her. Devil could not offer the real answer, that he did not trust himself to remain in proximity to her without being tempted to touch her. That her scent had been driving him to distraction.

That if he had to envision hell, it would likely be an eternity of being stuffed into a settee next to Lady Evie Saltisford, having a view straight down her bosom as she read Shakespeare to him, unable to touch her.

But nay, he could say none of that. He held her gaze. "Because I want to."

Milady was not appeased. "You must sit nearer. I have no wish to yell as I read."

He was not terribly far away. Far enough he could not catch her scent on the air. Sweet, luscious fruit. He was never going to eat an apple again without thinking of her, damn the woman to perdition.

Devil shrugged, saying nothing.

But Lady Evie was stubborn. "If you want to hear what happens next, you will move nearer."

He cast a glance about the library, searching for her lady's maid, who always seemed to have her nose in her embroidery and sat in a faraway corner. Once, he had sworn the woman had been snoring. This evening, she was nowhere to be found.

"Where is Smithson?" he asked, his voice sharper than he had intended.

Two golden brows arched. "She was not quite feeling the thing this evening, so I sent her to bed early."

An unexpected surprise, that. Milady cared about her servant's welfare?

Something shifted inside Devil's chest. He longed to beat on it with his fist and force the unwanted change to reverse itself.

Instead, he swallowed. "Kind of you. Best if I stay here."

Fuck. He had said too much. He gripped the arms of his chair and ground his teeth.

But his curt explanation was not good enough for her. He read it well enough in her expression, the sudden way her chin tipped upward, her spine straightening.

"Why?" she demanded. "Have I offended you in some

manner, Mr. Winter?"

Inwardly, he counted to ten and tried to distract himself. He could not respond with truth.

You have not offended me at all, my lady. But if I sit next to you again tonight, breathing in your sweet scent and looking down your bloody dress, I am going to want to do something we will both regret.

Nay. Couldn't say that.

Instead, he made a noncommittal noise deep in his throat. A sound of dismissal. A sound he hoped would tell her to read the damned play and leave him in his miniature chair. The contraption was pinching his arse. Had it been fashioned for children?

"I am afraid I could not hear your response, sir," she said smoothly, her tone lacking the sincerity of her apologetic words. "Likely because you are seated so far away."

The outrageous baggage.

Someone ought to turn her over his knee.

Not Devil. Though the notion of raising her gown and petticoats to expose her bottom was not an unfamiliar thought. He may have pondered it on previous occasions, sometimes in the darkest ink of the night, when he was alone in his bed, cock in hand.

He swallowed. "Read to yourself if you prefer."

Her full lips thinned with displeasure.

Could it be that she enjoyed reading to him as much as he delighted in the sound of her husky voice and clipped, aristocratic accent bringing him the unfolding story?

"I thought we had called a truce, Mr. Winter." Her voice was steeped in disappointment.

Even more interesting. He tried to keep the heat threading through him at bay and failed. *Damn, damn, damn.*

He found himself speaking again. "Were we ever at war,

milady?"

She pursed her lips now, emphasizing their plumpness. He had to stifle a groan, because that mouth. *Bloody hell.* It was made for sin. For wrapping around a man's—

"You told me you do not like me," she pointed out coolly.

"*After* you said you did not like me."

"You were glaring at me, and you are a large, intimidating man."

He shrugged, because he had a suspicion the gesture would annoy her, and said nothing.

She liked that less. Milady rose with the majesty Devil imagined any queen would possess, snapping the volume closed. "Good evening then, Mr. Winter. I shall see you in the morning."

That was it? She was retreating without a fight? Devil shot to his feet as well, for even rats like him, to the rookery born, knew to stand in the presence of a lady when she stood. Mayhap except his sister Genevieve, but that was a different tale entirely. Gen would box the ears of any man who did not treat her as if she were a lad.

Lady Evie whisked past him, holding his gaze as she went. Devil knew he ought to let her go. It was safer. Better. Why did he give a bean what happened to Romeo and Juliet?

But as she moved, elegant and ethereal despite her dudgeon, he caught the scent of ripened apple. He reached out, watching as if a stranger were in control of his own body, as he caught her elbow. Her warmth scalded his palm. Nothing but smooth, creamy skin. The softest flesh he had ever touched. Her silken cap sleeves did not descend far enough to cover her arm, and the shawl she had worn earlier had been abandoned on the settee. No barriers. Just his skin on hers.

She stopped and turned toward him.

He had never wanted to feel a woman's lips beneath his

more. Not even Cora had inspired such a raw, real, insurmountable depth of feeling. But he would not kiss Lady Evie. She was not his sort. She was betrothed to a foppish lord. He was here to protect her.

"Read," he ground out.

"READ," DEVIL WINTER ordered her.

His hand was on her arm. His bare skin on hers. The touch was potent. Not at all forceful or strong as she would have expected from a man of his size. But gentle. Something strange and warm slid through her, landing in her belly. She froze.

Mayhap baiting him, urging him to sit near her, had been a mistake.

Because everything inside her changed.

She had been aware of him before, but what she felt now went beyond that. What she felt now was…intoxicating. Thick and heavy. Hot and insistent.

"You have changed your mind?" she asked, voice low.

Giving her away, she feared.

Instead of releasing her, he trailed his fingers down her forearm, his thumb caressing the sensitive flesh of her inner arm. He stopped when he reached her wrist, his long fingers encircling.

His eyes were on her mouth. He was impossibly tall, towering over her. But if she rose on her toes, and if he ducked his head, their lips would meet. She could kiss Devil Winter. Longing surged through her. Before Evie could contemplate what she was doing, she swayed toward him, rising on her slipper-shod feet.

For a heartbeat, she swore he was going to seal his mouth

upon hers.

But then he blinked and released her as if she had scalded him, dropping her wrist. He nodded toward the settee. "May as well see what happens to Juliet."

As if he could hardly be bothered to listen. Disappointment surged. Had she been imagining his interest? After all, they were both trapped here, at this townhome for a fortnight, the sacrifice of her sister and Dominic Winter's overprotective natures.

She winced.

He was still watching her carefully, and he frowned down at her now. "Is your wound paining you?"

Her wounded arm was the opposite of the one he had touched. But his concern performed the same strange feats his touch had, causing tingles to sweep over her. "My wound is healing nicely."

He had inquired about it each day. Her lady's maid had been helping her to apply the salve he had provided.

He nodded again, saying nothing, his bright-blue gaze still lingering on her.

She flushed beneath the force of that stare, her cheeks going hot. Why did he suddenly have her so ill at ease? Her reaction to him was confusing. Shameful.

You must think of Lord Denton, Evie.

Yes, she had a betrothed. A golden-haired, elegant gentleman who would never growl at her or count her paces. Who treated her as if she were fashioned of the most delicate porcelain. Who had never tried to kiss her either.

On that rather vexing realization, Evie spun away from Devil Winter, putting some much-needed distance between them. What in heaven's name was she thinking, comparing a rough-hewn, illegitimate man born on the streets to Viscount Denton, the heir to an earl?

She seated herself on the settee and flipped the volume of Shakespeare open to the place where she had finished reading the night before. She felt his presence nearing her before his tall, powerful form cast a shadow in her lap.

Still, she would not look at him, for fear of what he would see reflected in her countenance. For fear of what she might so foolishly say or do next. Wordlessly, he settled at her side, careful to tuck his large frame as close to the opposite end of the settee as possible.

She was regretting her prodding, her invitation for him to sit here. He had done what she wanted, and yet she was more adrift than ever. Because his scent was teasing her senses, and out of the corner of her eye she spied the impressive muscles of his thigh, delineated by the dark breeches he wore.

With a deep breath, she plowed forward, reading more of the scene where they had left off. But keeping her mind on the play proved nigh impossible with Devil Winter seated at such proximity. His even breaths seemed to linger in the air like a wicked caress.

There was a heaviness in the room. A strange sense of change she could not quite define. But if she could not understand it, she could, at least, ignore it. So she did, turning her attention to the next scene in the play, Juliet in Capulet's orchard.

She had not read long when Mr. Winter interrupted her.

"*Take him and cut him out in little stars*?" he repeated, his tone incredulous.

Evie glanced up from the pages, her gaze settling upon him once more. "That is what Juliet said, yes."

"After he is dead," Mr. Winter added, as if he required clarification.

"*Give me my Romeo*," she read again, "*and, when he shall die, take him and cut him out in little stars—*"

"Worse than a body-snatcher, this bit of petticoats," Devil grumbled, interrupting. "Dangerous, too."

She searched his face for any hint of laughter, but found none. "She is in love with Romeo, and quite desperately so. Only listen to the rest. *And he will make the face of heaven so fine that all the world will be in love with night.* Is it not romantic?"

Mr. Winter snorted, his disdain evident.

"She is convinced all the world should love Romeo as she does."

A dark brow rose. "Plotting about his death and turning his body into stars?"

"A figure of speech, Mr. Winter. Nothing more." Evie paused, sighing. "I admire her devotion to Romeo. To have that kind of love must be an incredible gift."

"Until you're turned into stars." He sniffed.

"I should like someone to think of me in such memorable terms. To believe if I were turned into stars that I could make all the world fall in love with night." When she noticed the manner in which Mr. Winter watched her—the sharpness in his gaze, the stillness in his posture—she wished she could withdraw those words. Wished she could unsay them.

"Your Lord Dullerton does not?" His query was low. Gruff.

His stare was intense. Intimate.

It took Evie a moment to realize he had referred to Lord Denton as Lord Dullerton.

"His name is Lord Denton, Mr. Winter."

"Sounds the same to me."

She frowned at him. "I assure you, there is a marked difference."

But he was undeterred and unapologetic. "You didn't answer the question, milady."

Her cheeks went hot, for she realized she had just admitted aloud the secret she had been carrying deep inside her heart. The one she had not dared to share with anyone else; not even her twin sister Addy: that Lord Denton did not love her and she did not love him. Their sister Hannah had suffered a loveless marriage that had left her in agony. Evie did not want the same for herself. And Addy's marriage with Mr. Dominic Winter was…unusual. Scandalous to many. However, Addy and her Mr. Winter loved each other, madly and deeply.

Was it wrong to want that sort of love herself? To long for a love like Romeo and Juliet's?

"Milady?" he prodded.

She did not want to answer him. Not only because she had just made a most unhappy realization about her future with Lord Denton. But also because revealing her true feelings to Mr. Winter felt far too intimate. Every bit as intimate as the unexpected sensation of his hand on her bare skin.

"Shall I read more?" she asked, instead of giving him the response he wanted.

"No."

They stared at each other. His silence was deafening. His gaze shrewd. She could not shake the feeling he saw to the heart of her. Saw everything she did not want him to see. Everything she had not seen herself.

Until now.

Until this man.

He was dressed like a gentleman, but his cravat was an ornamented knot. His clothing was fine, of excellent construction. His particular branch of the Winters may have been born to the rookeries, but they had ultimately grown their wealth. She could almost look upon him now and imagine he was a lord.

Except no lord would be so large, his hands so roughened by manual labor. His stare so direct, his manner so lacking polished charm.

"Can you read, Mr. Winter?" she asked him suddenly, giving voice to the question which had been running through her thoughts ever since she had begun reading to him.

Ever since his reaction to her remark about his ability to count, in fact.

She had not intended to blurt it just now, but mayhap it was a manner of deflecting his attention away from herself and subjects she had no wish to discuss. His jaw hardened, his gaze sharpening. She regretted the rude query, but it was too late to recall it.

"No."

A lone, clipped word was his sole response. Nary a hint of emotion. No trace of anything on his impassive face, either.

Instead, Evie was the one whose cheeks went hot with shame, for prodding this proud man into an admission he may not have wished to make. She struggled to find something—anything—she could say, to allay the damage she had done.

"Forgive me, Mr. Winter. I did not intend to—"

"No need to apologize. I ain't a fancy lord. I can't read. There's no schooling for bastards raised in the East End to Covent Garden whores."

There was no anger in his voice, and yet she still flinched. "I am sorry, Mr. Winter."

"I ain't." His lip curled. "Read to me if you like, Lady Evangeline. Or don't. Time is wasting."

A hollowness blossomed in her heart, spreading. "I could teach you."

He stared at her, once more solemn and silent.

"To read," she elaborated, feeling foolish and yet needing

to continue. To make amends. To erase the damage she had so rashly done. "I could teach you to read, Mr. Winter. Whilst we are both trapped here with little else to entertain us, it may prove an excellent diversion."

"Is that what I am to you, milady?" he growled. "Entertainment? A diversion?"

"No." She shook her head, needing him to understand for reasons she did not dare comprehend. "I want to teach you, if you wish to learn."

"I don't need the charity of a duke's daughter."

"It is not charity," she bit out, frustrated with him, with herself. "I want to teach you, if you wish it. And in return, you may teach me a skill unfamiliar to me. Think of it as an even exchange between the two of us."

The two of us.

How those words lingered. How the thought lingered. Her cheeks went hotter still, and yet she refused to avert her gaze. To look away. To surrender. She held his stare. Blue burned into her, bluer than the summer sky. He was astoundingly handsome, Mr. Devil Winter, and Evie had never been more aware of that fact than now.

"You want me to teach you a skill," he said, doubt dripping from his baritone.

Did she? The prospect seemed ill-advised. Dreadfully so, as Mr. Winter teaching her anything would require a great deal more time spent together. So, too, her teaching him how to read.

And yet, the notion of spending more time with him did not perturb her in the least.

"Yes." Her answer left her before she could think better of it. "I will teach you to read, and you teach me a skill of your choice."

A wicked grin curved his lips.

Good heavens, when Devil Winter smiled, he was lethal. He stole her breath. She did not think she had ever seen a man as irresistibly, magnetically attractive.

"What if the skill I choose is not proper, milady?" he asked.

Heat flared in her belly, between her thighs, telling her she would not mind.

However, she fixed him with her most disapproving stare. "Mr. Winter."

"Knife fighting?"

She blinked. "I cannot imagine I would require such a skill."

"Pistol shooting? Fisticuffs?" he carried on.

"Whatever you wish, Mr. Winter," she relented, because she felt she owed him that much.

"Anything?"

There was a distinctively wicked note in his voice.

Everything, she longed to say.

More heat slid through her. She could not seem to keep her gaze from his lips. They were so full and thick. Tempting.

Nay! What was she thinking?

"Milady?"

His question sliced through her tumultuous thoughts. She forced her eyes away from his mouth. "Any skill you wish to teach me, Mr. Winter, as long as it is suitable for a lady."

There. He could not misconstrue her words.

Even if she wanted him to.

He nodded. "An even exchange. Whittling. That is what I shall teach you, Lady Evangeline."

For some reason, she wished he would call her Evie. But she wisely kept that thought to herself. They had crossed enough boundaries as it was this evening.

"Whittling, Mr. Winter?" she asked.

"I can carve almost anything you'd wish from a hunk of wood."

"A snowflake?" she suggested.

"Aye." He nodded. "I could make a snowflake with ease, and I can teach you to carve one as well, if you like."

"Yes. I would like that very much, Mr. Winter." She smiled at him. "You see? An even exchange."

He shrugged and maintained his stony silence.

Leaving her with no recourse save to continue reading where she had left off. She took up the volume of Shakespeare once more. "*O, I have bought the mansion of a love...*"

Chapter Five

LADY EVANGELINE SALTISFORD teaching him to read was Devil's idea of hell.

She hovered at his elbow, her nearness filling his head with fire. The scent of ripe apple would forever give him a cockstand from this moment forward. Her finger traveled slowly over the page, moving beneath the letters he was supposed to be reading.

At the moment, he could not concentrate on a single bloody thing outside the tempting swell of her bosom, hovering perilously near. He was jealous of his own damned elbow, which was the closest portion of his anatomy to her breasts. Terrible travesty, that.

"Say the word with me, Mr. Winter," she urged softly.

He could not force his attention to the page. Instead, he allowed himself the luxury of studying her profile. Her nose turned up ever so slightly at the end. A smattering of freckles was scattered on the elegant bridge. Her lashes were darker than her burnished curls.

"Romeo," he guessed. That one appeared often enough on the page.

"Romeo starts with an R, Mr. Winter." She glanced at him, and he realized her eyes were not brown at all. Rather, they were an exotic blend of gold and mahogany, with flecks of cinnamon.

Fuck.

What was wrong with him?

"Juliet," he guessed next.

Her lips pursed. It required all the restraint he possessed to keep from kissing her.

"There is no letter J in the word," she said softly. "If you truly wish to learn to read, you must at least try."

That was the crux of the matter. He did not want to learn to read. What he wanted to do was hoist her over his shoulder and carry her away to his chamber. Then, he would take those soft lips for his own and get her out of that pale-pink gown.

"Where is your lady's maid?" he asked.

"Smithson has the afternoon to herself today," she said.

How the hell was he expected to keep his hands to himself with temptation a hair's breadth away and no damned lady's maid presiding over these lessons?

"Isn't proper," he growled, irritated with her for continually appearing in his presence, unchaperoned.

She blinked. Then blinked again. Finally, her lips curved into a smile. And then she laughed.

Warmth trickled through his chest. My God, the throaty sound of Lady Evangeline's laughter stole his breath. And ability to think. Longing slammed into him, fierce and intense.

He swallowed past the steadily rising knot in his throat. "What is so bloody funny?"

"You fretting over propriety."

"Why shouldn't I? I'm here to protect you." Including from himself, which was apparently growing more and more necessary.

She stared at him, her expression turning pensive. "You seem rather stiff today, Mr. Winter."

She had no bloody idea.

He bit the inside of his lip and said nothing.

"Is something amiss?" she pressed.

He forced himself to look away from her lovely face. To the book that was open on the desk before them. To the word her forefinger still rested beneath. But even then, he could not concentrate on the typeset word, the ink printed upon paper. All he could look at was *her*.

Even her nails were elegant. Smooth and rounded, with a sheen no woman who worked with her hands could ever manage, the nails long rather than cropped short. They were not roughened and reddened like the hands of the other women he had known.

He should not be thinking of that lone finger trailing down his chest. Or her dainty hand wrapped around his cock. But there was something about Lady Evangeline Saltisford that made him think about everything he should not.

And then think about it some more.

"Are you ashamed?"

Her query startled his attention back to her. She was watching him with an expression that was part curious, part sympathetic.

His lip curled, because he would not be pitied. Not by her. Not by anyone.

He raised a brow, as if he had not a care in the world. "Ought I to be?"

"Of course not." She paused, seeming to search for the right words, mayhap realizing there were none. "Forgive me, Mr. Winter. I am going about these lessons all wrong, I fear."

Yes. Yes, she was. For one thing, she needed to be on the opposite end of the room. For another, she needed to wear a gown that buttoned to her chin. She also needed to stop smelling of fresh, ripe fruit. And looking at him with those big, brown-gold eyes. And to never touch him. *By God*, also to never again utter the word *stiff* in his presence…

"The lessons are perfectly fine," he gritted. "The problem is me. My mind. It does not comprehend reading."

"Give yourself a chance, Mr. Winter."

He could not stifle his bitter laughter at her optimism. "And why should I give myself a chance when no one else ever has?"

She frowned at him. "I am giving you a chance."

"Why?"

Lady Evangeline blinked, confusion furrowing her brow. "Why would I not, sir? We are together beneath a shared roof, bound to spend the remainder of this fortnight together. I find you are not as disagreeable as I once supposed you to be. Indeed, you are quite affable when it pleases you to be."

Affable. A fancy nib's word, that.

Yet another reminder his world and milady's could not be further apart, even if they were currently inhabiting the same space. Everything was temporary. When their fortnight of banishment was at an end, he would return to the East End rookery where he belonged. And she would marry her Lord Dullerton.

"Not as disagreeable as you supposed," he repeated grimly. "And affyble, aye?"

"Affable," she corrected him gently. "Forgive me. That was discourteous of me. I meant to say I…like you, Mr. Winter."

She…liked him.

Lady Evangeline Saltisford. Daughter of a duke. Blonde beauty. Diamond of the first water. *Liked* him.

Devil stared at her, at a loss for how he might offer proper response. The need to kiss her thundered through him, brash as any storm. He tamped the desire down. Ignored it. Had to. There was no place for desire here. Lady Evangeline would wed her Lord Dullerton. He would carry on guarding and protecting The Devil's Spawn. They came from different worlds.

Like Romeo and Juliet. Wasn't going to end well for either of them.

He stared at her, searching her face. Committing it to his memory, in truth. There would come a day, all too soon, when he would not see her with such regularity. When he would perhaps never see her again. The knowledge was a physical ache, tearing through him.

"Have you nothing to say, sir?" she asked softly, plumbing his gaze with her deep, mahogany-and-honey stare.

He had been silent again, he realized. All too often, he held his tongue in a show of power. He had learned long ago that what was left unsaid could be more powerful than words. But when he was silent with Lady Evangeline, more and more, that lack of speech was down to the way she made him feel instead.

He did not like it. Not one damn bit.

But he liked *her*. Far too much.

The last time he had allowed himself to feel anything had been with Cora.

He inhaled sharply at the reminder. "You *like* me, milady?"

Her cheeks went pink. He could not look away. When she was flushed, she was more beautiful. What must it be like, to have such a woman to call one's own? He had never in his life coveted what another man had before. Not even Devereaux Winter, who had been born on the right side of the blanket. The legitimate heir to their sorry sire's empire. But part of him raged at Dullerton making Lady Evangeline his wife.

"I do not think you as vexing a man as I once supposed,

when I first met you," she said softly. "There is far more to you than you allow anyone to see and know, I suspect."

The urge to wrap his hand around her nape, pull her mouth to his, and claim it as his own was strong. Strong and mad in equal measures. He had no business longing for a proper lady.

"Not as vexing as you supposed," he repeated wryly, though he knew he should not.

Knew he ought to leave it alone. To leave her alone. To do everything in his power to dispel this ridiculous desire pulsing to life within him. Entirely unwanted. Wrong in every way.

She caught her lower lip in her teeth, then released it. "You are misunderstanding me, Mr. Winter."

"Am I?" He studied her, giving no quarter. "How?"

"I like you. Not because you are no longer as vexing as I supposed. Not for any other reason than yourself. Forgive me for suggesting otherwise. I find you to be a most agreeable companion."

A most agreeable companion.

As if he were a duenna. A governess. Someone in a gown and petticoats seated in the corner of the room instead of a man thrice her size who was drowning in unexpected—and unwanted—desire for her.

He shot to his feet, needing to be anywhere other than near her. "Thank you for the honor you pay me, my lady. Your *most agreeable companion* has had quite enough of lessons for today. Mayhap we can try again tomorrow."

But when he would have departed from the study in which they had found themselves for his cursed reading lessons, a small hand on his arm stayed him. *Hers.* On a growl, he turned back to her, ready to unleash his displeasure.

Her countenance had him stopping, turning back to find

her watching him, her expression stricken. Her heart was in her eyes. And what a heart it was. Unscarred, unscathed. Whole and untouched, ready to be broken. But not by Devil. Never by him. Her husband would shatter that heart for her, likely within the first month of marriage. Lord Dullerton would turn to his mistress, and milady would be left crying into her pillow.

Why should he give a damn? It was the way of the world, cruel and cutting, rife with bitter disappointment.

"What?" he demanded, feeling churlish. Feeling as if his skin were suddenly too small for his body, as if he had been dipped into flames.

"Do not go, Mr. Winter."

Her sweet entreaty irritated him. Because it burrowed inside his chest. Reached him in a way no woman had. Not since Cora. The two women had nothing else in common. Cora had been dark-haired, bright-eyed, and impossibly sweet.

Until her sweetness had fled her.

And until *she* had fled *him*.

"No more lessons today," he snapped.

He was beyond his limits. Feeling things he had no wish to feel. Thinking thoughts he had no right to think.

With that, he shrugged free of her touch and from her presence altogether. He stalked from the room, leaving her behind him, all too aware of her stare on his back as he went.

SHE HAD DISPLEASED him somehow.

Evie watched Devil Winter's long-limbed stride taking him from the study, a feeling of helplessness overcoming her. She had intended to help him. To spend some time with Mr. Winter, understand him, get to know him. Instead, she had unwittingly chased him away.

And she hated it.

Loathed the way his handsome face had closed. Detested the hardness that had come into his sky-blue eyes, the tension in the bold slant of his jaw. Despised anything and anyone who made him feel inadequate, or as if he could never measure up to a peer of the realm.

She chased after him before she realized what she was about, catching his arm. Staying his retreat. He turned toward her, his expression thunderous. The man was not pleased. Through his jacket and shirt sleeve, his warmth burned into her. She removed her hand.

But Evie was not a wilting flower. She tipped her chin up, met his glare with a bright smile she little felt.

"Do not forget this is an even exchange, sir. You have promised to teach me your skill as well," she reminded him.

Not because she had any desire to wield a blade against a hunk of wood. But because she did not want him to hide himself away. Because she wanted him right here. With her.

Evie would worry about the meaning of that later. Devil Winter intrigued her. He…

Nay, Evie! Cease all such inappropriate thoughts at once.

She must not travel any further down that ruinous path. Mr. Devil Winter was not for her. She was going to marry Lord Denton, who was the epitome of elegance and polite manners. He was handsome, sought after, a most eligible *parti*.

Not as handsome as Mr. Winter.

She banished the unwanted, wicked voice. Even if it was true, she had no right to be entertaining such thoughts. Devil Winter was not for her. He could never be for her. Her sister may have married beneath her, wedding Mr. Dominic Winter in a bid to ease their madcap brother's gambling debts. But although their union had turned into a love match, Evie was firm in her path. Lord Denton was perfectly polite. He danced well, was the heir to a noble title, and her father approved of him.

Pity she was not in love with him.

However, love would grow. She was certain.

Devil Winter was watching her intently now, fixing her with a stare that yet again seemed to see far too much.

"You want to learn to whittle *now*?" he asked, as if the mere suggestion irritated him.

His voice was curt, angry, with an extra edge. Quite probably, she ought to tell him she had changed her mind. That he could teach her to carve another day. But the plain truth was she did not want to watch him go. She did not want to be alone.

Without him.

"Yes," she suggested brightly. "I do want to learn."

Something flashed in his eyes. Changed his expression. "I haven't the patience to play your teacher today."

An unfamiliar urge rose within her, a tightening in her belly, a heat flaring where it should not. The longing was fierce and insistent, foolish and wild, brazen and reckless. But it would not be quelled, no matter how hard she attempted to ignore it.

Mayhap it was that he was so handsome, so tall and strong and different from the gentlemen she knew. Or that he was there, within her reach. She felt connected to him in a way she could not explain. She felt safe with him, it was true. But she also felt…curious. Was it *Romeo and Juliet* that had her heart leaping and the rest of her feeling fluttery? Or was it Mr. Devil Winter?

Evie met his gaze, holding it. "What if I do not wish to learn how to whittle today? What if there is another sort of lesson I want instead?"

He stilled. The air hung heavy, rife with a poignant note. "What other lesson, milady?"

There was a dangerous note in his voice. His jaw tensed. The blue of his eyes deepened. His stare dipped to her mouth. The hunger between them was palpable, stealing her breath.

What was she saying? What was she doing?

She needed to cease this madness at once. She was treading on dangerous ground. Dreadfully unstable, rotten floorboards that could give out at any moment, sending her hurtling to the floor below.

She did not care. In the past few days, everything had changed. Every facet of her life had altered. The desire to feel this man's lips on hers surpassed every other need or thought.

She held his gaze. "Kissing."

Devil Winter said nothing. For a moment, she wondered if she had spoken that lone, forbidden word aloud, giving voice to the temptation.

But then, at last, he spoke, his voice deep and strong. "Kissing."

Her heart was pounding so loudly she feared he could hear it where he stood.

"Yes." Her voice was a whisper of sound as it left her.

"I cannot give you that sort of lesson, Lady Evangeline."

Stinging humiliation swept over her, chasing the heat, the awareness. She had made a grievous mistake. What had she been thinking to suggest he teach her how to kiss? She was engaged to Lord Denton.

But she had never felt a modicum of what she felt in Mr. Winter's presence for her betrothed. There was no comparison. How could she feel the way she did with a man who was not the man she was marrying? Indeed, with a man who was not a gentleman at all?

She swallowed down a knot rising in her throat. "Of course, Mr. Winter. I…do not know what came over me. Forgive me."

How mortifying.

This time, she was the one who was fleeing. She swept past him.

But before she could make good on her retreat, he growled, "Wait."

She turned back to him, staving off a rush of tears pricking her eyes. "I have already apologized, Mr. Winter. What more do you—"

The remainder of her words were silenced beneath his lips.

Devil Winter was kissing her.

Chapter Six

DEVIL HAD COMMITTED many sins in his life.

Kissing Lady Evangeline Saltisford was but one.

But none had ever been this bloody satisfying.

Her mouth was soft and ripe beneath his. For a moment, she did not move. She simply held herself still, her lips compressed. Her lack of response nettled. He tugged her closer, until their bodies were aligned. Her breasts crushed into his chest. The fullness which had been taunting him ever since their lessons had begun, unspeakably erotic. His cockstand, which had been raging throughout their interactions as well, rose to ruder prominence, pressing against her belly.

Her hands fluttered to his shoulders. Her lips parted. A sweet, husky sigh emerged from her into their kiss, and he swallowed it down. Greedily took it as his. He planted one hand on her waist and lifted the other to cup her cheek. Silken. Her skin was sleek as velvet. Everything about her was fine, dainty, elegant.

Fire raged through him. Need roared.

But he forced himself to go slowly. He had believed gentleness was not in him. His hands were massive paws, and he had inherited his worthless sire's broad shoulders and impressive height. He had never felt more like a hulking beast than he did as he held Lady Evangeline to him and kissed her.

She felt delicate and rare. And he was undeserving. Nothing but a rat from the seediest rookery in East London.

But still, he kissed her. Because he could not stop.

And even had he wanted to cease this madness—which of course he did not—her arms crept around his neck, holding him where he was. Anchoring him to her. Belatedly, it occurred to him that he had not kissed a woman since Cora. There had been others after her—nameless, faceless means of slaking his lust and swallowing his pain. But he had never placed his lips on theirs.

He sucked on Lady Evangeline's plump lower lip, then kissed the upper bow before pressing his mouth to the corners of hers. Now that he had begun, the urge to kiss her everywhere—to kiss her ceaselessly and never cease—rose, mad and strong within him. Her scent enveloped him. Ripe apple and honey-sweet woman.

He allowed himself further liberties, though he knew he ought not. His tongue slid past her parted lips to stroke against hers. Tentatively at first, and then with greater ardor when she responded in kind. The carnal wetness sent a new arrow of lust directly to his prick. The need to be inside her was so potent, he almost surrendered and picked her up in his arms to carry her to the nearest bedchamber.

However, though he thought he had rid himself of his conscience long ago, the bastard insinuated itself in the next moment, reminding him he could not go on kissing Lady Evangeline Saltisford. Her lips had never been his to take. She was a lady, quality, the innocent sister of Dom's wife, by God. He had to stop himself now.

Summoning every bit of his inner strength, he tore his mouth from hers. But still, though he knew he should thrust her away from him, put as much distance between them as possible, the rest of him did not want to let her go any more than his mouth had. His hand was still on the curve of her waist, the other cupping her cheek.

Let her go, you daft prick.

Her eyes were dazed and wide, dark. Her mouth the deep-red of crushed berries. She was the most beautiful sight he had ever beheld, and he wanted her with a ferocity that could have crushed his soul if he believed he still possessed one.

"Your lesson," he forced himself to say.

Then stepped away. Releasing her. His hands balled into fists at his sides to keep from touching her again. He was not the sort of man a woman like Lady Evangeline Saltisford wanted. Not the sort she would ever accept. Whatever madness had propelled her into suggesting kissing lessons from him, she would regret it.

She would regret *him*.

Just as Cora had, and Cora had been no fancy lady, no duke's daughter. Ladies did not want bastard Winters unless their hands were forced, as Lady Adele's had been. She might have gone soft and given her heart to Dom after the fact, but Devil knew the truth for what it was.

"I am afraid that was not good enough."

Her voice shook him from his thoughts, bringing with them a stinging sense of confusion. She did not think his kiss was good enough? Is that what the baggage was telling him? He could not believe his ears. Nor his eyes.

"Not good enough," he repeated, aware his voice resembled a growl more than anything.

Lady Evangeline Saltisford brought out the worst of him, it seemed.

Before him, she transformed, shoulders going back, defiance radiating from her along with that cool elegance she had. That duke's daughter boldness.

She held his gaze, keeping him trapped more effectively

than a man thrice his size. "I require more instruction, Mr. Winter."

Milady had returned.

He did not know which urge he ought to obey first—the one to kiss the chill from her mouth or the one to turn her over his knee.

Neither. That was the correct answer to such a troublesome question. To such an impertinent female. To a lady who tested him and tempted him in equal measure. *By God*, if this nonsense kept up, he was going to have to seek out Dom. Someone else would have to play the guard for milady. Blade could do just as well as Devil. He was the one who had killed to earn his bread until finding Dom and Devil.

"More instruction?" He glowered at her, summoning all the force of his fury, that rage he had kept carefully within himself all these years.

But this slip of a girl scarcely took note. She certainly showed no sign of fear.

"Surely you cannot deem what just transpired adequate."

There she went again with her duke's daughter words.

"Seemed fine when you moaned into my mouth, milady," he told her cruelly. Cuttingly.

Still, she showed no sign of retreating. "Why do you call me that?"

"You're a lady."

"You say it with such bitterness," she said. "You run it together. Never *Lady Evangeline*. Nor *Lady Evie*. Always *milady*, as if you are delivering an insult instead of paying a courtesy."

Not wrong, the persistent bit of petticoats.

Milady was a reminder to himself of who she was and what he was. If he had not been good enough for the likes of an East End girl like Cora, he sure as hell was not going to dally with the betrothed Lady Evangeline Saltisford. No good could come of it. A bad halfpenny is what this cursed nonsense was.

"You want to learn how to kiss for your nib husband?" he prodded. "Lord Dullerton could not do the job, aye? Too busy kissing his ladybird?"

He regretted the scorn in his words when she paled, recoiling as if she had received a blow. He had been trying to hurt her, to wound her where she would be vulnerable, and he had succeeded. The knowledge did nothing to pacify the bitterness roiling through him.

"His…ladybird?" She frowned prettily.

Despite her agitation, there was nothing he wanted to do more than kiss her until she couldn't bloody utter a coherent sentence. He stood before a crossroads. He could do the honorable thing and pretend he did not know a single damned detail about Viscount Denton.

But that was not the truth. Part of keeping themselves in Tip Street at The Devil's Spawn—swimming in coin—was knowing the details about all their patrons. Every detail. All the duns, the vices, the games, the ladies who warmed their beds, the favored spirits, how many times they pissed in a day.

Well, mayhap not that detail. But every other one there was to be had.

The choice was there—the road that would cause Lady Evangeline less pain and allow her to continue on in her ignorance. Or the road that would tell her the truth, painful and dreadful though it was. Gazing into her eyes, he chose the only path he could. The truth.

"The actress, Mrs. Hale," he elaborated. "His mistress. Lord Dullerton too busy kissing her to see his own betrothed properly kissed?"

He ought to have kept the last to himself, but he was

feeling vindictive toward old Dullerton. And covetous. Nibs did not know what they had. That nib in particular. If Devil had a woman like Lady Evangeline to kiss, he would never know another's lips.

Fuck.

Where had that come from?

"Mrs. Hale, the most celebrated actress in London?"

Celebrated for her prowess treading the boards and in the bedchamber both. Her beauty paled in comparison to lady Evangeline's. There could be no comparison between the two women. Lady Evangeline was beautiful, fierce, fiery, and surprisingly giving and passionate. She was not at all what he had initially supposed her to be. Mrs. Hale was pretty enough in her way, but she was also a woman who had lived a hard life. Her coldness showed in her eyes, and it was the hard stare of a woman who knew what she had to do to keep flush in coin.

"Aye," he said. "That one."

She cleared her throat, looking torn and pale and so unlike herself he wanted to kick himself in his own arse for allowing such rot to fall from his tongue. "She is Lord Denton's…ladybird?"

"Last I heard." Guilt lanced him. "Matters change, especially when a lord is expecting to take a wife."

The last was a blatant falsehood. Lords did not stop seeking cunny elsewhere when they wed. Rather, they grew bolder. The wife was for heirs. The mistress for pleasure. Nothing stopped them from taking what they wanted, however they could have it, unapologetically.

Which was also why Devil and his siblings unapologetically reclaimed the largesse of the quality who frequented their establishments.

"You are telling me Lord Denton has a mistress."

Lady Evangeline's voice cut through his thoughts.

He could lie to her. Or he could tell her the truth. He was not certain which of the two would land him in more trouble at the moment.

"If common fame is to be believed, yes," he responded.

And he knew it was. But he kept that salient bit to himself.

"Mrs. Hale."

"That is the one, aye."

Her nostrils flared, her full lips thinning and compressing in a betrayal of her emotions. For a moment, he wondered why the hell they were devoting so much attention to Lord bloody Dullerton. And then he recalled. She intended to marry the blighter.

"Mr. Winter?" She moved toward him, bridging the distance once more, bringing with her that scent he could not seem to resist.

What the hell was any man betrothed to Lady Evangeline Saltisford doing dallying with a woman like Mrs. Hale? One was a good-hearted innocent and the other was a cynical jade. He understood women like Mrs. Hale. They were women like the one who had given him life, who had to earn their living rather than having it provided for them. They were cunning and bold, using anyone they could to better themselves. Women who would sell their own sons to the demons of hell without a qualm if it meant something for them. One less mouth to feed.

"What is your Christian name?"

The gentle question shook him from his thoughts of the past. "Devil."

Lady Evangeline shook her head. "Your true Christian name. I do not believe anyone would name their child Devil."

His name hovered on his tongue, and he did not know

why. He answered to Devil. Devil was his name. It may not have been the name the woman who had birthed him had given him, but it was the name she had always called him. Later, he had embraced it for different reasons. He was no longer the weak lad she had birthed and abused.

He gave Lady Evangeline a grim smile. "Wrong, milady."

"Your true name."

What was the harm?

"Theodore." The name, so foreign and unfamiliar, one he had not claimed in years, left his tongue. Hung in the air. Suspended.

"Theodore," she repeated.

Heat flared in his chest. And lower. On her lips, he did not mind the hated name quite as much. But then, on her lips, everything was better. Sounded better. Tasted better.

He was bloody well doomed. If she asked him for more kissing lessons, he could not deny her.

DEVIL WINTER'S NAME did not suit him, Evie thought. Far too fussy and proper. Devil Winter was a man who was wild and bold and strong.

A man who had just told her she was promised to wed a gentleman who had a mistress. Mistresses were not suitable conversation for ladies to broach with their future husbands. She would have never done so. However, she would have liked to believe Denton would have been clear with his intentions for their marriage. Clear enough that she would have known he planned a traditional society union.

Which was not at all what she wanted.

And any guilt she may have felt at enjoying the kiss of another man was decidedly washed away by the reminder that her betrothed had never once set his lips upon hers. Meanwhile, he was kissing one of London's most famed actresses. And doing only heavens knew what else with her as well. Supposing she could believe Mr. Winter's word, that was. Certainly, he could be lying.

But such prevarication on his behalf now hardly made any sense. What did he stand to gain? Nothing, as far as she could see. She had already kissed Mr. Winter and all but thrown herself at him in embarrassing fashion. Besides, men like Devil Winter did not marry women like herself. That her twin sister and Mr. Dominic Winter were happy now was almost an impossibility. Their disparate worlds colliding in harmony—the rookeries of the East End and Mayfair—never happened.

And yet it had for Addy. Evie could not suppress the sudden, most unbecoming surge of jealousy accompanying that thought. Suddenly, true love—Juliet's love for Romeo and his for her—seemed far more important than any society match Evie could ever make.

"Mr. Winter is fine," he growled. "Or Mr. Nothing."

She regretted having called him the latter now. How cool she had been to him initially. Because she had been quite wrong about him, she thought. And intensely irritated at having to hide herself away, as if she were a shameful secret. Also fearful of what would happen. It was not every day a lady found herself suffering a gunshot wound in Mayfair.

But that was neither here nor there at the moment, because Devil Winter was still near enough to touch, watching her in that way that said *keep your distance*.

"You dislike your name," she inferred from his response—the tensing of his jaw, the stiffness in his bearing, the curling of his lip.

"I dislike the woman who saddled me with it," he snapped.

"Your mother."

"The woman who bore me."

They stared at each other, Evie assessing, Mr. Winter attempting to resurrect his walls.

"What did she do to make you hate her?" she asked softly, though she was certain she ought not to prod.

"Not enough time in the day for the list, milady." He inclined his head.

His reluctance to reveal more of himself to her sent a pang of disappointment through Evie. Was she wrong to feel as if they had bonded in the last few days they had spent together? That the kisses they had just shared meant something?

For her, they had been revolutionary.

"Tomorrow, then," she suggested.

His lips compressed. "No."

"Why *Devil*?" she asked him, changing her tactic. "It seems a rather extreme name."

"Sends the proper message, don't it?"

"Does it not," she corrected him.

"Ain't having lessons now, am I, milady?" His voice was mocking, his eyes hard.

She was scratching beneath his surface, and he did not appreciate her efforts. She wondered how much of himself Mr. Winter had ever shared with anyone.

"I enjoy our lessons," she confessed.

"No more lessons, milady," he said gruffly. "Bad idea, and I should have known it. No use teaching me to read. And you kiss just fine."

"Fine," she repeated, dismayed.

"I've kissed better."

His cutting words, issued in his deep growl, insinuated themselves inside her heart, where they lodged like a tiny, painful splinter. She could not decide if he was being deliberately cruel because he wanted to flee her presence, or if her kisses had indeed been dreadful. It was a distinct possibility her kisses had been uninspiring, though she hated to admit as much.

Still, Evie was not about to allow him to see how much his callousness affected her. "I am certain you have, considering I have not had the practice one undoubtedly requires."

He raised a dark brow, the scar on his forehead lending him a menacing air. "And you imagine I *have* had the practice, milady?"

He looked as if he had had the practice. He was a dangerously handsome man. She could not countenance the notion of any lady not wanting to kiss Devil Winter. Particularly now that she had known his lips upon hers.

"Have you not, sir?" she asked, feeling bold.

Feeling as if someone else had overtaken her. Someone who dared to ask a wicked man like Devil Winter for kissing lessons and challenged him at every turn. Who made certain her lady's maid was otherwise occupied so she could be alone with him at every opportunity.

Yes, she had done all those things since her forced confinement at Mr. Devereaux Winter's townhome. An abundance of caution had left her with a dearth of it herself. She was catapulting herself into danger.

"Hardly any of your concern how many ladies I have kissed, is it?" he asked, his gaze traveling over her in a familiar fashion.

She felt that stare as if it were a caress.

Once more, she was aflame. Because Lord Denton had a mistress, and she was alone with a man who did not.

Or did he?

She frowned. "Do you have a ladybird, Mr. Winter?"

The word left her tongue with great difficulty. In part

because the notion of him having such a woman awaiting him filled her with dread, and in part because propriety and rules had haunted her each day of her life with a dogged persistence. Her mother, her governess, even her older sister Han, and her twin Addy—every female she had ever known from her ailing grandmother down—had impressed the importance of maintaining an impeccable reputation.

"How is that your business any more than how many women I've kissed, milady?" he asked, cool and confident.

He had kissed her with such fire, and now he spoke to her with a distinct lack of passion. Was it because he was tempted as she was, or because her kisses had been a true disappointment? Oh, how she wished he did not fill her with such confusion.

"I suppose it is not," she agreed, feeling small. Terribly small. Tinier than an ant. "Once more, I must beg your forgiveness, Mr. Winter. I have kept you here long enough, forcing my whims upon you."

But instead of leaving as she had imagined he would, Devil Winter remained where he was, studying her with that sky-blue gaze that saw too much.

"Not force," he bit out, his words and his tone clipped.

Almost angry.

She blinked. "I beg your pardon?"

"You did not force anything upon me," he elaborated. "I...kissing you...'twas not a chore, milady."

Not a chore.

She could not stifle the bubble of laughter rising within her, almost hysterical. Would his insults know no end?

"Not a chore? Next you shall tell me kissing me is not as dreadful a task as emptying chamber pots."

He winced. "Christ."

"I do think you are right, sir. We ought not indulge in

any more lessons of any sort," she said on a rush, hoping to get out the words before humiliation swamped her. "I am sorry for imposing upon your time and…mouth. I shall not repeat the insult. Good day, Mr. Winter."

"My lady…"

She did not want to hear another word more. Evie was feeling foolish and furious and sad, all at once. She had managed her first kiss, but to a man who apparently had found little enjoyment in it. And she was betrothed to another who was wooing a mistress but had never attempted to so much as kiss her lips.

Evie held up a hand, silencing him, and then she dipped into a curtsy and fled.

Chapter Seven

DEVIL FINISHED CHECKING in with the men he had charged with watching the perimeter of the townhome. He made his way back to his chamber using the servants' stairs, determined to get an early night's worth of sleep. To get any sleep at all, as it happened. The last two nights had been plagued with thoughts of *her*.

He gritted his teeth and tamped down the reminder to settle his mind upon the task at hand instead. He was not meant to lust after his charge. He was meant to protect her. And protecting her thus far had proven far easier than before, now that they had moved to Devereaux Winter's spare home.

The reports from his men had been excellent. Nothing had changed. No suspicious persons had been seen. All had been quiet. Another week and this nonsense would be over. His duty to Dom would be done. He would persuade his brother that everyone would be far better served with Devil returned to his post. If the Suttons had indeed been behind the shots which had been taken at Lady Evangeline, Devil would find out everything there was to know. He would discover who, why, and he would bloody well end them.

And then, milady would be someone else's problem.

He ought to be relieved.

Except, the sensation roiling in his gut at the moment was not relief at all. Because as much as he relished his days at The

Devil's Spawn, presiding over the staff and aiding Dom in making certain all their family businesses ran smoothly, he had to admit, he had *enjoyed* spending time with Lady Evangeline.

Which was why he had been spending as little time in her presence as possible since their lessons exchange had descended into pure Bedlam. The best sort of Bedlam. But altogether *wrong* Bedlam.

Kissing her had been a mistake. He never should have done it. She was not for him. She was going to marry a nib. And he was nothing like a nib. He was as far as one reasonably diverged from a fancy bloody lord.

But her mouth. Lord above, fucking fuck and all the saints and angels, *her mouth.* Having it beneath his for a few moments had been worth every bit of penance he would have to do. And anyway, he had committed enough sins for two men. What was the harm of one more? So long as he never repeated it…

Dom would kick his arse if he found out Devil had been playing at kissing lessons with his wife's sister. Hell, Devil wanted to kick his own arse for the stupidity he had been indulging. He certainly had a knack for lusting after petticoats who could never be his.

On an irritated sigh, he opened his chamber door and slipped inside. Darkness greeted him. Unlike other evenings since he had reluctantly taken up residence at yet another Mayfair mansion, the manservant who kept a brace of candles burning for him had failed to do so.

The moment Devil crossed the threshold, the hair on the back of his neck rose.

His senses never failed him.

This time, they were alerting him to the fact he was not alone.

Someone else was in his chamber, waiting for him, hiding

in the cloak of darkness. His hand went to the hilt of the knife he kept hidden in a pocket sewn into the lining of all his coats. There was also another tucked into his boot for the same purpose.

Tense, ready for a fight, he moved slowly, treading deeper into the chamber, the plush Aubusson silencing his footfalls. A floorboard creaked, giving away the location of the unseen intruder.

If Sutton had finally sent someone to murder Devil, he was far too late. And he had also chosen the wrong man for the task.

"Mr. Winter?"

The hell?

Had he lost his mind, or was the trespasser in his chamber Lady Evangeline?

He stopped, still gripping the hilt of his blade. "Milady?"

The scent of succulent, sweet, ripe fruit hit him.

It was her.

He sheathed his knife and stalked toward the direction of her voice. "What are you doing here in my chamber, in the dark?"

Damn her. Could she be any more trouble? If she was not occupying all his thoughts, then she was here, in his chamber. Where he could touch her. Or kiss her again. Both actions which he must avoid at all costs.

"I wished to speak with you."

"You could have done it all bloody day," he growled, furious with her for invading his chamber. Even more furious at what he could have done to her, had she failed to say his name…

The mere notion made his stomach churn with violent upheaval. He found his way to the tinderbox and struck away at the flint. His irritation proved a boon for the task. In no time, he had the brace of candles lit, filling the modest chamber he had taken with warm, golden light.

A dreadful mistake, as it turned out.

Because milady was wearing a night rail.

A thin, virginal white affair buttoned to her throat. But it clung to her curves as if it had been fashioned for the sole purpose of tormenting any man who gazed upon her whilst she wore it. It was the sort of gown a man could not help but to imagine tearing off her.

Her eyes were wide, lower lip caught between her teeth. "I wanted to speak with you alone. That could not have been accomplished by any other means than awaiting you here."

He withdrew his knife, candlelight glinting off the sharp blade. "I could have stuck this between your ribs, milady. That's what I was about to do, when you spoke."

Her gaze settled on the knife, her pallor undeniable. "I…did not think of such a possibility. Forgive me."

"You may have been born to ballrooms and silk, but in the rookeries, when a man is hiding in the darkness, there's only one reason for it. He intends to kill you, and you've got to draw your blade first and sink it deep."

She frowned. "I did not want the servants to know I was in here awaiting you. I thought it would be easier to hide myself if one of them were to return if there was no light. I did not think…"

"Aye," he bit out, losing his patience. "You did not think, did you, milady? You never do, else you would not commit half the reckless actions you take."

The expression on her face only filled him with further fury. She looked stricken.

Damned spoiled duke's daughter. He threw his knife. It hurtled through the air, the blade landing in the wall on the opposite end of the room exactly where he had intended, the tip buried inside Devereaux Winter's fine plaster. He would pay for the repair to the wallcoverings later. For now, he was too damned irritated to care.

Her lips parted as her gaze went to the blade protruding from the wall and then back to Devil. "There is no need to be so rude, Mr. Winter. I was not hiding in your chamber with the intention of doing you harm. I only wished to talk."

Talking was the last thing he wanted to do with this vexing baggage.

What he *wanted* to do was kiss her breathless. And then strip her bare and bury his face between her thighs. To lick her until she was writhing and desperate and spending all over his tongue. But he was not going to do any of those things, damn it. He was going to get her out of here instead. Latch the door behind her pretty back.

"I do not want to talk with you, milady," he growled at her. "And you do not belong in my chamber."

"How else was I to garner a moment of your time? You have been avoiding me for the past two days."

Had he been avoiding her? Hell, yes, he had. Because kissing her had been the height of stupidity. And he had thought of nothing other than doing it again ever since.

"You have been in my presence plenty," he gritted. "You could have said what you wanted at any time."

Despite his surliness, milady showed no signs of relenting. She remained where she was, stubborn as ever. "Not in the presence of Smithson."

He had made certain to never be alone with her since those disastrous lessons. Her lady's maid had been playing the chaperone, keeping them both out of further trouble. Now she was here, where he had spent every night stroking his cock to thoughts of her.

Shite, damn, fuck.

All the curses in the world were not sufficient to adequately express the way he felt this moment.

"Anything you have to say to me would be best spoken before your lady's maid," he rasped, hating the huskiness in his voice, giving him away.

A river of lust was flowing through him. Threatening to carry him away.

"I want to resume our lessons," said the cursed woman.

The lust river turned into an ocean. He was drowning.

Devil closed his eyes and counted to ten. But when he opened them, she was still standing in his chamber, her brown-gold eyes fastened upon him, her face unutterably lovely.

Wearing a night rail.

And that was when he noticed her nipples were hard. Tempting, stiff buds calling to him from beneath that linen.

He jerked his gaze back up to her eyes, where it was far safer to look. "No."

The persistent wench did not flinch. "Why not?"

"Get out of my chamber."

If he was going to have to toss her over his shoulder to bodily remove her, he would. She could not bloody well remain standing here, with her nipples taunting him. He was not fashioned of stone, although he had no intention of bedding her.

"Mr. Winter," she began.

"No," he interrupted, not interested in hearing anything else she had to say.

"Theo," she tried again.

She had not just called him Theo, damn her. No one called him that.

"Devil." He was moving forward now, propelled by his ire and his increasingly waning ability to restrain himself.

Her eyes widened, but she did not retreat. Instead, the impossible woman remained where she was, bare feet firmly planted on Devereaux Winter's expensive Aubusson.

Even her dainty feet were alluring, curse her. Devil had never noticed a woman's feet, for God's sake.

She smiled. "I prefer Theo."

So did he when she said it in her sweet voice. *Hell.* That smile of hers did indecent things to him. He reached her, folded his considerable height in half, and settled his shoulder into the softness of her belly as he wrapped his arm around her legs. There. He straightened, and she was light as a bird, slung over him.

"Mr. Winter!" she shrieked.

Too loudly, by God.

He swatted her rump. "Quiet or you'll bring the house down upon us."

"That stung, you brute."

A brute, was he? Good. Mayhap if she thought ill of him, she would do a better job of keeping her distance.

Devil turned on his heel and retraced his steps, saying nothing.

"Put me down! I want to speak with you. Why are you carting me out of your chamber? Theo! Mr. Winter!"

The more he ignored her, the louder her protests became. He swatted her bottom again. A bit harder this time. Damn, her arse was an excellent handful.

"Devil!" she spat just as he reached the door.

He stopped. "Curse you, lower your voice."

"Fine. Put me down and I will speak in a quieter tone."

"It is not my reputation I seek to protect, milady."

"Why are you so eager to have me removed from your chamber?" she demanded, sounding outraged.

"If you looked in the shiner, you would know," he told

her grimly.

"Shiner?"

"Looking glass," he bit out. She had him so distressed, he had failed to realize he was using cant.

"You object to my night rail? I do suppose I ought to have worn a dressing gown atop for modesty's sake, but I was in a hurry."

For modesty's sake.

Was the woman a Bedlamite or just incredibly innocent?

"Quiet now," he ordered her. "We are about to go into the hall."

"I shall shriek as loudly as I can if you do not put me down this instant."

The manipulative minx.

Devil thought about giving her rump another swat before ultimately deciding to settle her on her feet once more. He glowered down at her, keeping his gaze trained upon hers. He was not going to look at her damned nipples poking through the fine fabric of her night rail, begging to be sucked…

Fuck.

He looked at them. How could he not?

His cock went harder than a fire poker. He stalked past her to his bed and snatched the counterpane from it before wrapping it around her shoulders. "There. Now you may speak, milady."

For good measure, he took two steps in retreat. She was no longer within reach. *Excellent.*

"I am not cold," she pronounced, milady in full force.

He ground his molars. "Say your piece before I toss you over my shoulder again."

"There is no need to be a bully, Theo."

Was she trying to make him tear out his hair? Did the woman take pleasure in his torment?

"Devil," he bit out, moving nearer in spite of himself.

"You are certainly behaving the part." She pursed her lips, and the urge to cover them with his rose, impossible to be denied. "However, I do prefer Theo. It is so much more civilized than—"

The final thread of his restraint—frayed beyond repair—snapped. He pulled her near, cupped her face, and lowered his mouth to hers, effectively silencing her.

HE WAS KISSING her.

Again.

Mayhap it was wrong. Certainly, it went well beyond the bounds of propriety. But then, so did appearing in a gentleman's bedchamber in the darkness, wearing nothing more than a night rail. And she had done that. Because she could not bear the distance that had suddenly occurred between them.

A distance which was no longer present now.

Her hands went to his broad shoulders, the movement causing the counterpane to fall to the floor. His lips were firm, insistent, and hot. Moving over hers with an expert precision that made her melt.

His tongue traced the seam of her lips, coaxing her to open for him. And open she did, on a sigh. There was no way to explain the change that came over her when this man kissed her. She had never imagined the act could be one of such intimacy, that his lips on hers could make her feel such an unprecedented range of sensation and emotion.

Here was what she had been missing from her life, and she knew it now, instinctively. Knew it even as the notion terrified her.

This man.

Theodore Winter. Devil Winter. By any name, her reaction to him was the same. The effect he had upon her staggering. She never would have thought it possible.

But she needed to be nearer to him now.

She was not close enough.

Rising on her toes, she entwined her arms around his neck. She pressed her breasts to the sturdy wall of his chest. Against her belly, a prominent ridge rose, thick and enticing, making a corresponding ache blossom to life between her thighs.

Just as quickly as the kiss had begun, however, he ended it, tearing his lips from hers and thrusting her away from him with such haste she nearly tripped over the discarded counterpane. But his strong hands caught her arms, helping her to maintain her balance. Searing her skin.

She looked down at the sight of his hands on her, and that was when she noticed the ink marking on his inner wrist, one she had previously not observed. Black and shaped like a blade, the mark looked as if it had been drawn upon his skin.

"Steady," he told her, sounding as breathless as she felt.

She wondered for a moment if he was issuing the command to her or to himself. His blue stare was deep and intense, making her giddy. He released her once more in haste, as if she were fashioned of flame that would burn him.

She reached for him, her fingers tracing over the inking on his flesh for just a moment before withdrawing. "What is this?"

"A blade," he said. "My sister Genevieve drew it. We all have them."

How intriguing. Evie had taken note that her sister's husband also had a similar marking on the top of his hand. It would seem each of his siblings had one.

"Your sister is talented," she said, taking note of the attention to detail on the hilt of the dagger.

"I cannot help but to think you did not seek me out to speak of my sister," he drawled, the coolness in his voice making her suppose he was completely unaffected by the kisses they had just shared.

The only sign otherwise was the hint of a flush on his sharp cheekbones.

"You are correct," she forced herself to say. "I came here to speak with you about our lessons."

"Our lessons are over."

She raised a brow, saying nothing.

"That was not a lesson just now," he bit out. "That was stupidity."

His dismissal stung, but she was determined. "I want to continue them."

"No."

He seemed to forever be telling her that word. "Why not?"

"No good can come of their continuation."

"Do you not wish to learn to read?"

"We cannot be alone together."

"We are alone together now," she pointed out.

"Not for long," he growled. "You were just leaving."

But when he moved as if he intended to throw her over his shoulder once more, she danced away. "You cannot remove me, Mr. Winter. I want to speak with you, and speak with you I shall."

"Damn it, wrap the counterpane around you."

Why was he so insistent about the dratted blanket? She had not seen herself in the looking glass—the shiner, as he had called it—but she was reasonably certain she looked the same as she always did. Blonde hair, upturned nose, mouth too wide. Her night rail was quite modest.

"No," she said, deciding two could play at his game.

His response was another growl.

"Theo." She tried the name again, rather liking the way it felt, the way it sounded. Yes, it suited him far better than Devil. "Do try to be reasonable. We have another week here, and I shall suffer from terrible ennui if you do not give me the lessons you promised you would."

His expression was all hard angles and planes. He looked furious.

"Which lessons?" His voice, however, was silky and smooth.

Something wicked unfurled inside her. "You know which lessons."

He remained implacable. "You teach me to read, and in return, I teach you how to whittle."

"I had in mind a different sort of lesson from you," she admitted.

Because it had occurred to her over the past two days that she was engaged to be married to a gentleman who had a mistress. A gentleman who had never once inspired in her a modicum of the feelings this man made her feel. If she could not have a love like Romeo and Juliet's, then mayhap she could have a passion like theirs instead.

Mayhap she could have Theo Winter, if only just for the next sennight.

They could not have each other forever, much like in Shakespeare's tragedy. However, they could have now.

"Not going to happen, milady," he said, dashing her hopes. "I ain't a nib, and I don't poach."

Drat him, why did he insist upon being so firm? He was not as impervious as he pretended, she swore. His kisses had suggested quite the opposite.

"Why not?" she asked, summoning all her daring.

"That's like asking why the stars and the sun don't shine at once," he said, his tone gentling. "We are not the same sorts, milady. Not of the same world. And you will be marrying your Lord Dullerton soon enough."

Evie did not bother to correct his confusion of Lord Denton's name this time. She was still quite furious with him for Mrs. Hale.

"I suppose I shall have to find someone else willing to engage in lessons with me, then," she said, trying a different tactic. "Mayhap one of the footmen will do. The tall one with the blond hair is rather handsome."

"You will do nothing of the sort."

She shrugged and then spun to leave.

A hand caught her elbow, staying her retreat.

She glanced back at him to find his jaw tense, his eyes blazing with blue fire. "How do you propose to stop me?"

"Damn it, Evie."

At last, he had called her Evie as she had asked him to the day when she had been wounded and he had been tending to her injury. Her name in his deep baritone, even edged as it was with a combination of irritation and anger, made warmth pool low in her belly.

"Yes?"

He had the counterpane in hand once more, and he draped it over her shoulders without relinquishing his hold on her elbow. "Do not tempt the devil."

"You are not the devil, Theo," she told him softly, hating the manner in which he seemed to view himself, as if he were a bad man or somehow inherently wicked.

Her every interaction with him thus far suggested otherwise. He was so much more than she had initially supposed, and now that he had given her a small peek at the man beneath his gruff exterior, she only wanted to see and know more.

"You do not know what I am thinking about now or you would change your mind."

His gruff words made more heat flare within her. Along with something else—longing, acute and intense.

"Tell me."

He shook his head, maintaining his silence, releasing her elbow.

Not fair. He could not issue such tempting hints and then refuse to share the rest.

"Theo."

"Whittling," he said. "That is the only lesson I will agree upon. Now return to your chamber and do not dare to set foot in mine again, milady."

Disappointment lanced her burgeoning hope. But then, if she could convince him to carry on with their lessons, that meant they would have additional time in each other's company. Hopefully without the watchful eye of her lady's maid. Yes, Evie could see she would have to create some distractions for Smithson. If they were alone, she was quite certain she could persuade him to kiss her again.

"Very well," she conceded. "I will return to my chamber, and I will agree to continue our lessons, as you wish."

"I do not wish," he growled. "You are leaving me with no bloody choice."

She smiled at his irritation, unable to help herself. What was it about Theo Winter that made him more handsome when he was irritated? Mayhap it was the way his upper lip curled. Or the way his eyes darkened. Perhaps it was the tensing of his strong jaw.

Oh yes, she would have him agreeing to more kissing lessons in no time.

With that thought, she dipped into a makeshift curtsy, clutching his counterpane around her. It smelled like him, she thought, and she was keeping it. He could find another.

"Good evening, Theo. Sleep well."

As she made her way into the hall, careful to make certain no servants were about, she swore she heard him grumble *not a damned chance of that.*

Chapter Eight

SHE WAS THE devil in petticoats.

He had never been more certain than after five more days of working together on their lessons. Her lady's maid was once again otherwise occupied today, leaving them alone. He was certain the devious minx had orchestrated something to keep Smithton busy just so they would be unchaperoned.

This time, she had copied some short sentences on paper. Her penmanship was neat and flowery, as he would have expected. The mark of a gentlewoman to whom every advantage had been given in life.

And she was seated beside him, smelling of ripe fruit and temptation. He had never wanted another woman more.

Not even Cora.

The realization had hit him when she had first crossed the threshold, sunlight gleaming in her burnished curls and roses in her cheeks. It had required every bit of self-possession he had to keep from stripping her out of her night rail and making love to her the night she had gone to his chamber. To stop himself from keeping her with him all evening long, showing her all the reasons why he could not offer her further kissing lessons, damn it.

Because once he started, he would not be capable of ceasing.

Desiring her had become his driving force.

He had spent half the long night every night since tossing and turning in his bedclothes, thinking of her, before finally surrendering and taking himself in hand. The releases had given him precious little relief, because he was still harder than an anvil by morning, and he still longed to take up where they had stopped when their lips had last met.

He wanted them beneath his now, more than he wanted his next breath. Actually, he wanted *her* beneath him now…

Dangerous thoughts indeed. Thoughts best avoided altogether.

"Do try this one, if you please," she told him, her voice soft and warm as her skin.

He could listen to Lady Evie speak all day and night long. He could also go on touching her and worshiping her body for a bloody eternity.

But neither of those thoughts were doing him one whit of good any more than the reckless ones which had preceded it had.

His days of practice with Lady Evie had taught him there were certain words he struggled with, also certain sounds. She made an excellent teacher, however, and her gentle tutelage, coupled with his rudimentary past knowledge, had painstakingly turned into something promising. Just as well, for their time together was almost at an end. Difficult to believe the speed with which the last fortnight had passed.

He would miss Lady Evie Saltisford. Would miss her luscious apple scent, her smiles, her gold-brown eyes, her generous curves, and…having her near. *Christ.* What was the matter with him?

He forced his attention back to the words on the page she had written out for this lesson, struggling to make sense of the letters before him, strung into words and sentences. To follow the loops and swirls of the ink. To find meaning. Damnation, trying to read was not much different from trying to make sense of the way Lady Evie made him feel. Both seemed nigh impossible.

But try he would.

"The," he read haltingly, his ears going hot with acute shame as he revealed the extent of his inability to her. "The… ball… stared to roll."

Made no damned sense. Not any more sense than the way he felt about her did. A lady. Finer than Cora had been. Out of his reach. Betrothed to a fancy nib who would never appreciate her the way she deserved.

He sighed.

"Excellent work, Theo," she praised, beaming at him as if he had just conquered all the world for her and laid it at her feet as spoils. "But try this word again, if you please. Sound it out slowly to make certain you are seeing *all* the letters."

He tore his gaze from her beautiful face and pinned his attention back to the paper and the words she had written. "The… ball…st-ar-ted to roll." This time, he understood the sentence. "The ball started to roll."

There. He had read a damned sentence, and it made sense this time, when he took care and sounded out the letters. Mayhap he was not as witless as the woman who had birthed him had always claimed. The only reason she had been able to read was because her father had been an apothecary and had taught her to help him with his ledgers. But when Devil labored over the words slowly, taking care to watch each letter and recall its sound, he could actually read a few words strung together.

"Wonderful!" Lady Evie exclaimed, her approval making other places go hot. Not just his ears.

His cheeks, for one. His heart for another. And as for the warmth sweeping to his ballocks, well, that could hardly be denied either. She was fetching and…sweet. Two words he had never supposed he would associate with milady at their first meeting.

"Will you try another?" she asked, her tone coaxing.

She was being patient and kind in a fashion no female before her ever had, showing him the sort of compassion he had only previously experienced from his siblings. He ached with the need to kiss her. To take her in his arms, the paper and the words she had written upon it be damned.

He glanced down at the next line, because he did not just want her approval. He wanted to bask in it. He wanted to make her proud, to prove to both her and himself that he could read.

Because he could. He suspected he had been capable of reading all along, but the mockery of the woman who had raised him still rang in his ears and landed in his chest like a vicious thorn.

"I…have…a kiss f-f—" He stumbled over the word, struggling.

"Note the sounds," she encouraged.

"I have a kiss f-for you," he finished, a triumphant sense of accomplishment bursting open inside him, rather like a bud in full bloom.

And then he realized what he had just read.

The scandalous bit of baggage.

"You have a kiss for me?" she asked.

She was smiling. The expression on her face could only be described with one word: pride. She was *proud* of him. She, an elegant lady as fine as any he had ever met, was proud of him, Devil Winter. Bastard son of a Covent Garden whore. Born to the rookeries, sometime buzgloak—the pickpocket who had robbed the pockets of fancy coves to fill his belly.

Another knot was rising in his throat, along with a foreign

emotion, lifting him up. Pride. In himself.

He swallowed against an unwanted rush of emotion. Something was pricking his bloody eyes, and he knew it was not tears because he did not cry. Not even when the man he and Dom had been sold to had attempted to hurt them. Not when he had acted first, defending them both with his quick thinking and his sharp blade.

"Theo?" she asked, her voice hushed.

As if she feared someone would overhear, when thanks to her, there was no chaperone to be found. No observation of propriety. Not that Devil gave a goddamn about such nonsense. Because he did not. Scandals and rules and polite society did not exist in the East End.

"You should call me Mr. Winter," he forced himself to remind her. "When our time here is at an end, you will forget me."

The smile faded from her lips. "I could never forget you."

He knew she was wrong about that. Cora had forgotten about him. Lady Evangeline Saltisford would as well.

"We come from two different worlds."

Her lush lips parted, and for a long pause, she said nothing, merely searched his gaze. "Your brother is married to my sister. Our worlds are connected by that bridge."

How he wished that were the truth. Because he was a fucking idiot.

"There will be no bridge you can cross to me when you are Lady Dullerton," he pointed out. "Lady Adele may be accepted because of your father and my brother's power. Your husband won't allow you to consort with the likes of me. I expect our paths will not cross after this."

She looked as stricken as he felt at the realization.

No more Evie in his life. No more golden curls, seductive scent, kind encouragement, sinful temptation. No more reading lessons or stolen kisses. The man he had become in her presence would once more cease to exist.

Which was just as well, for the Devil Winter who allowed a slip of a girl to know his true name and call him Theo was a Devil Winter who would bleed to death on the streets at the next attack from the Suttons. Or any enemy with a blade or a pistol. *Hell*, even Davy, the thieving little rascal Dom had taken in, could slit his throat in his sleep.

She had made him soft, Lady Evangeline Saltisford.

And another part of him astonishingly hard.

Damn, fuck, hell.

Still, epithets did nothing to quell his rampaging lust.

He inhaled slowly.

"Lord Denton shall not have complete command over my life after we are wed," she said, with all the naïve assurance of a lady who believed her nonsense. "I will be able to continue our lessons if it pleases me."

What manner of lessons, he wanted to ask. Reading or kissing? He suppressed the urge, telling himself she spoke of reading, naturally.

And then he bit out a bitter bark of laughter at the notion of her believing she could do as she pleased as Denton's wife without the lord being the wiser. "My lady, I can *assure* you that your husband will not allow any lessons between us."

She frowned. "Then I need not tell him."

He raised a brow. "You do not think he will know? Your servants will be his. Wherever you go, whatever you do, will be reported back to him. Suppose his servants inform him his wife is disappearing in the rookeries to teach a tremendous, uncouth beast how to read. Or worse. What would you do then?"

He would not describe their *other* lessons in greater detail aloud, for fear of the visceral reaction his body would have.

Also, some foolish part of him—the part that had not learned a goddamn thing from the hell Cora had put him through—refused to acknowledge the fact that Lady Evie was suggesting she would marry Dullerton and continue her lessons—presumably the reading sort—with him.

"You are neither tremendous nor uncouth," she said softly. "And certainly not a beast."

Breaking him. That was what she was doing. Cutting him with her kindness. Making him weaker still.

He brushed it all aside, forcing himself not to think of the inevitable end of their time together. Or her looming union to Dullerton, which felt akin to a blade in his chest. "I am all those things, and it would be wise of you to remember that. I ain't a nib. I'm the bastard son of a whore. You're the daughter of a duke."

"You are more than that, Theo. So much more. I wish you could see yourself as I do."

Curse her. He summoned all the ugliness within, years spent in the rookeries fighting for his life, for that of his family. Cora's betrayal. She'd had the opportunity to be his wife, and she'd chosen to be an earl's mistress instead.

"I do not need your pity, milady," he told her, maintaining his pride.

"I do not pity you. Nor do I see any reason why we cannot continue as we have. Indeed, after I am a married woman, I shall have more freedom than I have ever had."

His lip curled. "You truly think to continue our *lessons* after you are Lady Dullerton?"

Once more, he could not bring himself to directly mention the kisses they had shared, fearing his weakness for her would take hold.

"Lady Denton," she corrected primly. "Yes. Why not?"

Devil could think of a whole bloody list of reasons why

not. An endless fucking list of *why nots*. "Has it occurred to you that I may no longer require your lessons?"

The color fled her cheeks. "Because you will not wish to see me any longer?"

Something shifted inside him. It felt, for a brief, dizzying moment, as if the entire earth had moved. What was the matter with him? What had she done to entrance him as she had? He was already plotting ways their paths might cross, to the devil with his pride.

Wrong, all of it.

He had been down this ruinous path before. And he had emerged with a distrust of all women. A hatred of tender emotions and longing and lust, but above all *love*, that temperamental, fickle fucking witch.

A witch who would never again cast her spell over him as long as he lived and breathed. At least, that was what he had been telling himself until this golden-haired beauty had appeared in his life.

"Theo?" Lady Evie prodded, encouraging him to answer.

Reminding him who they were, where they were, everything that was at stake. So bloody much. More than he could have ever imagined. And at the height of it all, her welfare. He was no closer to discovering who had been behind the shots taken at her now than he had been a fortnight ago. But all too soon, he would have to say his goodbye to her, to wish her the best. Return to East London where he belonged and forget he had ever met a woman as wonderful as Lady Evangeline Saltisford.

He forced himself to recall her initial query. *Because you will not wish to see me?*

There would never come a day.

But he said none of that. Instead, he forced himself to remain calm. Cold. To be as impenetrable as he had supposed himself to be.

"Thank you for the reading lessons, milady. Now, it is my turn to deliver in kind."

What he meant was whittling lessons. Not that a lady such as herself would ever need them. A knife and wood—it was laughable, a duke's daughter taking on such a talent. *Hell*, even he knew ladies were taught to ply their talents in needle and thread. In the ballroom. In the drawing room. Ladies were fashioned of silk and satin and propriety. He was made of wood and iron and wickedness.

"How do you propose to deliver in kind?" she asked him.

Setting him more aflame than he already had been with her innuendo, blast her.

"Well, Theo?" Her gold-brown gaze had settled upon his lips. Her stare was a touch, a brand. "How shall you deliver?"

He forgot to fret about everything in that moment, about the danger lurking like a shadow, about her society's notion of rules, about what would happen later, about her becoming another man's wife. For a moment, she was his. They were the only two people in the world. And he could not stop himself from taking her lips with his.

The marriage of their lips was hot, sending a jolt straight through him. He pressed harder, thrusting his tongue into her mouth. He had missed her lips. He had missed her responsiveness, the way her generous curves melted against him.

She tasted of sweetness, sugar, tea, bergamot, *Evie*. Everything that was delicious. Devil barely suppressed a groan as he deepened the kiss, their bodies aligning. He wanted every part of him to burn into her. To remind her what she would be missing, what she would lose, when she became Lady Dullerton.

He ended the kiss before he lost control, tearing his mouth from hers. The thought of her marrying another made bile rise in his throat. He swallowed it down, forced himself to think of Cora and her betrayal.

"There," he forced himself to say. "Have I not delivered? Mayhap your Lord Dullerton will wish to thank me. If you will excuse me, milady. All our lessons are at an end."

Without waiting for her to respond, he stalked from the chamber, nettled with her. More furious with himself for the weakness he had for her. For being stupid enough to allow himself to want her. If Cora, who had been born to the rookeries as he had, had been too good to marry him, what the hell did he think would come of dallying with Lady Evie?

Nothing that was good.

Devil stalked down the hall, deciding it was time for him to return to where he belonged before he did something even more witless.

THE HOUR WAS desperately late. So late, the faint strains of dawn were lighting the sky where Evie had been keeping a window vigil in between frantic pacing of the chamber as the knot of worry in her stomach doubled, tripled, and finally quadrupled in size.

Theo had left their lessons without a backward glance earlier that day, and then he had left the townhome entirely. What was worse—he had yet to return. She knew because the window at which she stood, the carefully made bed behind her, and the chamber she had been pacing were all his. She had gone to his chamber after he had not accompanied her in the library as had become his habit to listen to the conclusion of *Romeo and Juliet*.

Without him there, Evie had not had the heart to continue on. It had not felt right. Nothing without him felt right.

She could not explain the change that had come over her this last fortnight. Devil Winter made her feel the way Romeo made Juliet feel. But she had no wish for their tale to be a tragedy.

She never wanted her fortnight with him to end.

But the evidence it already had was before her. Unless something had befallen him, which was worse. The healing wound on her arm throbbed, a constant reminder of the unknown danger swirling around her. If something had happened to Theo because of her, she would never forgive herself.

Evie bit her lip to stave off a stinging rush of tears.

The brace of candles she had lit hours ago was down to scarcely any wick and wax. She turned away from the shadows in the street below and paced the Aubusson some more.

Where could he have gone?

When would he return?

Before her troubled mind could continue whirling with any more questions, the door swung open at last. And there he stood.

A gasp tore from her.

His face was bloodied, his white cravat hanging loosely about his neck, also stained scarlet, as if it had been sprayed with blood. The linen of his shirt was similarly marred. A dark bruise colored the flesh beneath his left eye, rendering the blue more startling as their gazes clashed.

"Christ," he muttered. "What the bloody hell are you doing here? I told you never to come to my chamber again."

She swept forward as he kicked the door closed behind him without caring to blunt the sound. The portal slammed shut, echoing in the stillness of the night. The worry that had sunk its vicious teeth into her over the course of the night relented, but only a bit. He was injured. She had no idea where he had been, what he had done, or how he had received his injuries.

But he had returned.

He was here with her now, and that was the most important fact. She would fret over the rest later.

"What happened to your face?" she asked, not giving a care for propriety or the manner in which they had last parted.

She reached for him, rising on her toes to cup his face in her hands.

He winced. "Careful, milady. I'm a bit bruised."

"Where were you, Theo?" She searched his gaze, frantic for answers, heart thudding rapidly. "Have you been set upon by footpads? Are you injured anywhere else? How can I help you?"

As she fired off the questions, she made certain her fingers were gentle. They traveled over his jaw, finding a lump hidden by the layer of whiskers which had grown since the morning.

"Too many questions, milady." He winced again as her fingertips skimmed his cheekbone, where another purple bruise appeared to be forming beneath a cut. "And you have yet to answer mine. What the hell are you doing in my chamber? Again?"

If she were not so worried about him, mayhap she would have allowed the curtness in his voice to hurt her. However, after spending hours fearing the worst, she did not care if his tone carried the stinging lash of a whip. Her pride fled. He was all she cared about.

"I was here awaiting you, of course," she answered him primly. "Where have you been? Where did you go? I was worried about you."

"Worried about me." He released a bitter laugh, then winced when the action apparently caused him pain.

"You have cuts and bruises all over your face," she pointed

out.

All over his beautiful face. And despite the blood and lacerations, he was the most handsome man she had ever beheld. A rush of forbidden longing hit her as she held his face in her hands. Their lips were so near, his gaze fierce and intense upon hers.

"Aye," he said.

One word.

Low.

Dangerous.

There was an indefinable menace rolling off him this evening. All the tenderness he had shown her during the last fortnight, the gentle side he possessed, seemed to have disappeared. In its place was a stark, angry, wounded man.

Had she done this to him? Had she pushed him too far? Was this her fault?

"What happened?" she asked him again.

His lip curled. "Nothing for you to worry over, milady. I ain't your betrothed, am I?"

There was an edge in his voice she did not think she misunderstood. Jealousy. But surely not, from this enigmatic man who could not stop reminding her about the disparate worlds they inhabited.

"No," she agreed. "You are not."

Lord Denton was.

But you could be, she wanted to say.

Though she bit her tongue, she had come to a realization this evening as she had been pacing Theo's chamber. And it was that she no longer wanted to marry Denton. She wanted happiness. Love. She wanted a man who did not keep a mistress whilst professing his undying devotion to her.

She wanted Theodore Devil Winter. He was the Romeo to her Juliet. She just had to persuade him. And find a way out of her looming nuptials to Lord Denton. And convince her family—already outraged by Addy's sudden marriage to Mr. Dominic Winter—that her happiness was far more important than any match she could make or coronet she could snare.

But that was all going to have to wait for another day.

Because Theo was battered and bloodied. And it was nearly dawn.

"Get out of my chamber, Lady Evangeline," he told her coolly.

The dismissal in his voice should have cut her deeply. But she had not slept all night, and she had spent all the time since he had stalked away from her worrying over him, their relationship, their future. To the devil with tragedies.

"You missed the end of *Romeo and Juliet*," she told him, pretending he had not just ordered her to vacate the room.

Instead, she stroked a thick lock of hair which had fallen over his brow from his forehead.

He swallowed, and with his cravat untied, the subtle dip of his Adam's apple briefly riveted her. What a beautifully masculine throat he had. She wondered what the rest of him would look like, similarly bare. His chest. His arms. Lower…

"They're both going to die," he growled, and then he jerked from her touch as if she were a bee who had stung him.

It took her addled mind a moment to realize he was speaking of Romeo and Juliet. She frowned at him. "How do you know?"

"It is a tragedy." His lip curled. "Life is a tragedy. That is how it ends. And this is how *we* end, milady. Now return to your chamber with your innocence intact. One day you can entertain your grandchildren with the fable of how you once spent a fortnight with an East End rat and still lived to tell the tale."

"Life does not have to be a tragedy," she countered. "And you are not an East End rat. You are a gentleman with a kind and gentle heart."

He threw back his head and laughed as if she had just told him the greatest sally. "What rot. You amuse me, milady. Truly, you do."

He was trying to hurt her, she thought. Attempting to put as much distance between them—physically and emotionally—as he could. But she was not going to let him, damn it. She was going to fight him every step of the way.

Because she loved him.

The realization thundered through Evie with a physical jolt, as if she had been struck. Somehow, over the course of her fortnight with Theo, she had lost her heart. A heart she had once foolishly believed she would give to her husband in time. But it was no longer hers to give. Like Juliet, who had fallen desperately in love with a Montague when she was a Capulet, Evie had fallen in love with a man who should be forbidden to her.

She loved Theodore Winter.

Once, she had suspected Addy's mind of turning to pudding. Now, she suspected her own. It was the only explanation.

"Theo," she said softly. "Tell me where you went. Tell me what happened. Let me tend to your wounds."

He shook his head. "I told you not to come to my chamber again."

His eyes had darkened to a deep, stormy shade of blue. A flare of answering heat unfurled within her. "I was worried about you, Theo."

"Damn it, do I look like a Theo to you?" he roared.

His voice was like a crack of unexpected thunder. Evie flinched, taken aback by the fury in his tone, his countenance.

In this moment of raw, unadulterated emotion, he did not look at all like the Theo she had come to know. Instead, he looked the part of the raw, rugged East End gutter rat he purported to be.

But it mattered not to Evie. She loved that part of him, too. She loved all the facets of his personality. She loved his imperfections and flaws, for they made him into the man he was. Loved the scar over his brow, the inked dagger marking on his wrist.

"Yes," she told him firmly, "you do. You look like my Theo. Now do stop hollering, else you shall bring the entire household down upon us."

He blinked. "Milady—"

"Stop," she interrupted, raising her hand in a silent plea. "Call me Evie, if you please."

"Evie," he corrected with ease. "Get out."

Hmm.

One third of the words he had just spoken were excellent. The other two thirds, she would happily ignore.

She moved past him, approaching an elegant mahogany stand where a basin and pitcher were filled with fresh water. "I am not going anywhere, so you may as well cease fuming at me. You have cuts that need to be cleansed. I do hope you brought your salve along with you, for I fear you will need it for the wound on your cheek."

Tending to him was a much-needed distraction. It made her feel useful and necessary. It also made her feel less like crying. The sight of him in such a state was worrying. She hoped it was not because of her.

"I can tend to myself," he growled.

He was not going to run her off; she was determined. She poured water into the basin, found a cloth, and dunked it within, before wringing off the excess. Evie turned to find him standing where she had left him, his expression fierce, his gaze hard.

"I know you can tend to yourself, Theo," she told him calmly, "but you do not have to. I am here."

"Not for long."

His harsh words hit her heart like a handful of pebbles. Stinging pain, but she could endure. Evie ignored them.

She crossed the room to him and took his hand in hers, tugging him toward a chair. "Come and have a seat so I can better see you. You are as tall as a mountain."

And every bit as immovable. He would not budge from where he stood.

She pulled harder.

He glowered at her. "You are a little bee buzzing about a bear."

"Then you had best take care, lest I sting you." She pulled at his hand, noting it, too, was covered in dried blood, his knuckles swollen and cracked.

He did not wince as she tugged on his battered fingers, though surely the action must have caused him pain. "Bees ought to know better than to menace bears."

She found his wrist instead, warm and vital beneath his sleeves. Her thumb traced the smooth skin where she knew the inking of a blade hid. "Yet here I remain, foolish bee."

"Foolish bee indeed, to suffer the wrath of a bear." But as he said the words, he finally allowed her to tug him toward the chair.

He sat, looking distinctly unimpressed.

"You are neither bear nor beast," she said, studying his ravaged face. "Will you tell me where you were all this time or am I to be left guessing?"

"Home."

The curt answer made sense. She gently wiped the blood

from his cheek. "The Devil's Spawn?"

"Rookeries."

"Why?" She finished cleaning his face and studied him.

"Trying to find answers. Not going to find them here, playing lord and lady with you."

Playing lord and lady.

"Is that what we are doing, Theo? Playing?"

He said nothing, simply stared back at her. The bruise beneath his eye was darkening, giving him a menacing aura. One of the candles sputtered out. In no time, they would be in darkness.

On a sigh, she turned away from him, fetching fresh candles and lighting them with the remnants of the brace that had been burning all night. When each one was replaced, she took the bloodied cloth to the water basin and rinsed it, all too aware of Theo's gaze on her as she moved.

When she stood before him once more, she picked up his hand, tenderly cleansing his injured knuckles. "I am not playing a game. Not with you. Never with you."

He stiffened, tensing beneath her ministrations. "Evie—"

"Theo," she interrupted. "We have become friends over this past fortnight, have we not? And, dare I say, more than that, I hope."

His jaw clenched. "We cannot be friends or…more. Our worlds are too far apart. Look at me. This is who I am. Tonight, I beat a man unconscious with these fists."

He held up his hands, showing them off, one still covered in dried blood.

She swallowed. "Is that why you truly went to the East End? To prove to yourself we are too different?"

"I told you why. I need to find out who is responsible for trying to hurt you."

"Because you care," she said softly, taking his other hand

in hers and beginning to clean it as well.

"Because I no longer want you to be my problem." His lip curled. "So you can become Lady Dullerton."

He was trying to hurt her, doing his best to build a divide between them. But she was not going to allow him to do it. "What if I no longer wish to become Lady Denton?"

He rose from the chair abruptly, forcing her to take a step in retreat as he towered over her. "You do not know what you are saying, milady."

"I know what I am saying." She also knew what she was not saying, because it was too terrifying to reveal just now, when she was not certain of his feelings. "This fortnight has been a revelation for me. I have realized the marriage I was willing to settle for is no longer what I want."

What she did want was him. If only he would allow it. But she kept that to herself as well.

"And you know all this after a mere fortnight?" He gave a bitter laugh. "Only a cossetted duke's daughter would be so fickle."

"Stop thinking of me as a duke's daughter. Start thinking of me as a woman."

He made a low sound in his throat. Part growl, part grunt. "I have thought of you as little else from the moment I first set eyes on you, damn it. That is the problem. I do not belong in your world, and you have no place in mine. You have taken on the role of nurse remarkably well, but now your job is done. Go back to your chamber where you belong and get some rest."

How did he suppose she could sleep, leaving things between them like this?

"I will not go until you tell me what happened."

"Prizefighting."

"Boxing?" she repeated.

He shrugged. "I went looking for answers. When I'd gotten all the information I could, I stayed for a boxing match. Won fifty beans."

She supposed fifty beans was fifty guineas.

"You were not hurt because of me?" she pressed, needing to know.

"If you think I'm hurt, you should see O'Neal." He shrugged, as if fisticuffs, blood, and a blackened eye were of little consequence. "You've had your answer. Go to your chamber now. I'm tired and I need some rest."

She was not going yet. "You did not answer my question."

"I was not hurt because of you. The fight was for me."

"For you?" She searched his gaze, struggling to comprehend. "Why?"

"To keep me from touching you," he growled. "Now. Get. Out."

To keep him from touching her?

The change within her was happening again. Something was shifting in her heart. Melting and filling her with warmth. Love seeping into all the shadows, casting its undeniable light.

She held her ground, refusing to retreat this time. "What if I want you to touch me?"

Chapter Nine

HER QUESTION SET him aflame.

His cockstand was instant. The longing thundering through him so tremendous he forgot to breathe. It was bigger than him, overpowering, claiming his every good intention where Lady Evangeline Saltisford was concerned. Burning any shreds of honor he possessed into ash.

He would never know which of them moved first. All he did know was that one moment, she was standing before him, her countenance more vulnerable than he had ever seen, unfairly beautiful with her golden hair unbound down her back and a dressing gown to shield her modesty. The next, she was in his arms, and their lips were fused.

Soft, supple breasts collided with his chest. Her curves pressed into him, making his heart pound. Not even the rush he had experienced earlier when he had taken on Sean O'Neal in an impromptu bareknuckle match could compare. He was exhilarated. Fancy cove words. He blamed them on her.

He blamed everything on her, along with the fact he had discovered all the information he needed tonight in the East End, and the answers he had garnered meant by morning's light, they could put an end to this farce. He had already formed a battle plan on his way back to the townhome. Tomorrow, he would do everything he could to make certain Evie never again needed to fear for her safety.

But none of those facts could keep him from wanting her now.

Or from kissing her with everything he had.

He licked the seam of her lips. *God*, she was sweet. Sweeter than he deserved. Her tongue stroked against his as she welcomed his kiss, welcomed him. Her response proved his undoing. He was not going to take her. No matter what she thought she wanted, he knew better. The mere hours they had remaining was not enough time. There was nothing he could offer her save desire.

And he meant to give it.

Meant to make her quake and lose control, ache gloriously until she splintered into a thousand jagged shards of herself. Never mind his battered knuckles, his bruised face. He felt no pain. All he knew was the undeniable urge to taste her. Touch her. Bring her pleasure.

He broke the kiss and lifted her in his arms with ease. Her curves were generous, but she was deliciously short, and he was a big, muscled oaf. She felt as light as air. Perfect, tucked against him. As if she belonged. He wanted to keep her there forever.

But he could not.

He could only have tonight—*Christ*, this morning or whatever hour it was. Dawn had not yet broken, and the servants had yet to scramble into action. He had time. Precious little, but time enough.

He stalked toward the bed, his gaze riveted to her face. Flushed with passion, gold-brown eyes wide, lips swollen from his kiss. His. For the next hour and no more.

"You want me to touch you?" he asked gruffly.

"Yes." She did not hesitate in her affirmation, the throaty dulcet tone of her voice washing over him like a caress.

Fucking hell.

He had always known she was going to be trouble, from the first moment he had clapped eyes upon her. But he had never known just how much. How badly he would want her.

None of that mattered now. He laid her gently on the bed. "I let you tend me. It's my turn to tend you, my lady."

He was going to make her spend. If he could never have her again, at least he could know how she tasted. He could have her on his lips, tongue. Make her writhe and quake and come undone beneath him.

With trembling fingers, he unhooked the buttons lining the front of her dressing gown. If he had but one moment to savor her, he was going to see her, damn it. He was going to have the memory of her naked and glorious, awaiting him on his bed, forever imprinted upon his mind. She shrugged out of the sleeves and rose to her knees on the mattress, clad in nothing save another of her desperately taunting night rails. Together, they tugged the gown over her head.

For a moment, he lost the ability to speak. His tongue was sluggish and insufficient. His mind affected by a cloud of sheer, unrepentant desire. He inhaled the scent of ripe apples and sin and temptation. Evie. A goddess. More beautiful than his pathetic imagination had been able to envision.

Full, pale breasts tipped with hard, pink nipples. So much smooth, delicious skin. Wide hips, lush thighs, her mound covered by a thatch of golden curls. His mouth was watering. He was out of his mind. A Bedlamite. For as long as he lived, he would never forget the sight of her bare for him, awaiting him, his to pleasure.

"Lie down," he ordered her, his voice hoarse with the power of his need.

He was going to suck her pearl until she spent all over his tongue. And then he was going to do it again.

She did as he asked, lying back on the counterpane which

had been brought by a servant to replace the one she had thieved from him the night she had worn it about her shoulders like a cloak. She pressed her legs together, the flush on her cheeks deepening.

She was shy and innocent, his Evie. And bloody beautiful.

He joined her on the bed, daring to glide his bare palms up her calves, past her knees. Her skin was silken and creamy. He could do nothing but worship her. He lowered his head, pressed kisses along her inner thigh as he caressed her.

"Relax for me, love."

He coaxed her legs apart. Her thighs opened, revealing her to him. At long last. He had dreamt of this so many nights, he could scarcely countenance she was real. Her cunny was pink, glistening, and pretty. He could not wait another moment to have his mouth on her. Taking her hips in a gentle-but-firm hold, he found her pearl and sucked.

She jerked beneath him on a low, keening moan.

The taste of her was musky, sweet, flooding his tongue. He could not get enough. She was slick. So slick. He licked down her slit, his tongue dipping into the tempting cove he would not breach no matter how much he wanted to. Her hips pumped beneath him. *Bloody hell*, she was so responsive.

Desire roared through him, as intense as any longing for a woman he had ever felt. And he knew instinctively he would never again know this fervent need. This all-consuming yearning, which was so different from the lust he had known for others. Not just for her beautiful body, but every part of her, to her soul.

Her heart.

He knew it could never be his, but he was a greedy bastard when it came to Evie, and he meant to make the most of the precious time he had with her. Starting with making her unravel. Tentatively, he licked back to the bud peeking from between her folds. He flicked his tongue over her, lightly at first, giving her time to adjust. Learning what she wanted, what made her quiver and sigh.

Then he sucked her into his mouth once more, watching Evie as he pleasured her. A more glorious sight he had never seen. Words eluded him. She had risen to her elbows, head tipped back, lips parted. Her breasts were full and round.

He gently nipped her and her hips jerked, her gaze meeting his. What he saw in their molten depths spurred him on. He held her stare, nibbled at her pearl, and then sucked hard.

His name fell from her lips like a prayer.

Not Devil, but Theo instead.

When she called him Theo, he wanted to be that to her, for her. He wanted to be *hers*, damn it. And he knew without a doubt that whatever happened after this fleeting interlude, wherever he went, and regardless of whether she married another, he would be hers. Forever.

There it was. More dangerous longing for something he could never truly have. Stolen moments. This passion. That was all he could lay claim to. Her body, her pleasure. That was what he must settle for. The stars and the sun did not mingle. Night could never dwell in day. Romeo and Juliet did not grow old together. The children of the East End were born with the taste of bitterness and disappointment in their mouths. He should know that better than anyone.

And yet, part of him was desperate to believe there could be a way. That there could be more for them than these stolen pleasures.

There could not.

Even after the intimacies they shared, she would remain Lady Evangeline Saltisford. He would still be Devil Winter. There was no bridge between them, despite what she said before. Tonight had proven that. He belonged in the East

End. When he had returned, he had felt at home. He had pummeled his opponent with the aching hands that were now caressing her flesh.

He had to be the one to set her free, the one to protect her. And he would do that soon enough; as soon as he could.

But first, he would be the one to make her come undone.

He teased her with a finger, slicking her dew over her, then alternated between licking her swollen nub and sucking until her body was rocking into his. She undulated beneath him, her breathing emerging in breathy pants. He had to be inside her. If not with his cock, then his finger. Slowly, mindful of her inexperience, he dipped his forefinger into her opening.

Her tight heat gripped him, drenching him.

She was soaked. Her cries spurred him on, along with her body, surging up to meet him, dragging him deeper. He suckled her as he fucked her with his finger, a slow and steady rhythm. How he wished it was his cock she was clamped on. But the evidence of her steadily mounting pleasure was a reward all its own.

Curling his finger inside her and sliding deeper still, he worked her bud with quick, fluttering strokes of his tongue. She clenched on him suddenly, her body shuddering beneath him, her cunny pulsing with the force of her release. Her cream coated his finger, and she was somehow wetter still.

He pressed kisses to her mound, working the last strains of bliss from her. Her golden lashes swept over her brilliant eyes, shielding her stare from view. That was when he realized their gazes had held the entire time he had pleasured her. His prick was hard and long in his breeches, begging to be freed, desperate to sink inside her and feel her wet heat bathe him. To feel her welcome him into her body. To make her his in truth the way he was always hers.

He already knew the next mark he would ask his sister Genevieve to make upon his battered hide. An E for Evie.

"Oh, Theo," she said, her voice throaty and sated, her body limp and breathtaking on his bed, thieving his ability to say anything of reasonable intellect.

If indeed he had ever been capable. He supposed he had never been a man given to much speech until she had entered his life with the force of a storm.

He pressed a kiss to her inner thigh, gratitude surging within him. She had bestowed a tremendous gift upon him, and he would never forget this night. Would never forget her, even when she was far from him.

Her eyes opened, finding him, reaching inside him in a way only she could. "Do you think we might try that again sometime soon?"

He kissed down the rest of her thigh, then moved to the other, smiling against her silken skin though a wave of bitterness threatened to kill his desire. "We can do it again now, if you like, love."

"Now?" Her mouth opened, her tongue peeking out to run over the fullness of her lower lip.

He suppressed a groan at the sight, imagining that pink tongue of hers upon him, swirling over his cockhead. But it was not meant to be. Still, he could give her more pleasure. The sun was not yet risen. The servants would not be moving for another half hour or so. He could take this last opportunity to savor her before he was out of her life forever.

Devil lowered his head and sucked on her pearl once more. "Now," he murmured against her sodden flesh, before pressing a kiss there and then sucking.

"Mmm," came her telling response.

It was all he needed.

EVIE WOKE WITH a smile on her lips to what appeared to be late-morning sun filtering in through the window dressing of the chamber she had been occupying for the last fortnight. She stretched, still feeling deliciously sated and alive in places she had never imagined existed before.

Everything seemed the same.

And yet, everything had changed.

Theo had kissed her…between her legs. Her face burned at the memory of what he had done in those early-morning hours, but so too did the flesh he had pleasured. She was throbbing there, filled with a strange sensation of emptiness and neediness all at once. A desperation to know more. To feel his lips and tongue on her, his finger inside her, again.

Who could have imagined such raw, unadulterated joy existed? That such pleasure was possible? Certainly not her.

He had been so sweet and tender to her. After he had brought her to the heights of bliss three times, he had helped her to dress and guided her back to her chamber just before the servants had begun to roam the halls for the day. The way he had gazed down at her just before he had left her at the door to her chamber made her heart feel as if it had grown twice its size.

The walls he had continually built had been dismantled at last. He had pressed a kiss to her crown, wrapped her in an embrace. For a moment, he had simply held her, pressed tightly to his chest, his warmth and strength surrounding her. She had breathed in deeply of his scent, clinging to him as well.

All too quickly, it had been over.

He had disengaged and left her standing in the hall with trembling limbs and a pounding heart.

The door to her chamber flew open suddenly just then, interrupting her solitude.

But it was the person flying over the threshold that shocked her more than the intrusion. Addy was racing toward her, face a mask of worry. "Evie, how are you feeling, dearest sister? When Devil sent over a note that you were ill, I feared the worst."

Her lovely twin sister, the dark to her light, swooped down on her as if she were a mama bird, pressing a hand to her forehead. "You do not feel feverish. Mayhap the fever has broken."

Feverish?

Ill?

Theo had sent over a note?

The lovely sensations that had lingered as she woke were abruptly dashed as she blinked the remnants of slumber from her eyes and frowned at Addy. "Why are you here?"

"Is it a lung infection? An ague?" Her sister frowned right back at her. "Have you been coughing? I have had a poultice made for you to lay on your chest. How long have you been sick? Devil said it was quite dreadful, these last few days. You do not look pale, however. Indeed, you appear quite hale."

Suspicion colored her sister's tone by the time she stopped speaking. But the misgiving in Addy's voice was nothing compared to the doubt that was suddenly threatening to drown Evie.

"I am not ill," she told her sister. "Not at all. I am perfectly well, as you can see. What nonsense is that which you speak of?"

"Devil's note suggested it was quite grave, that I must come here at once…"

Addy's words trailed off as she appeared to make sense of the situation.

So did Evie. The walls which had been torn down had been erected once more. Only this time, he had built parapets atop them.

A stinging rush of pain seared her. "Where is he?"

She already knew the answer without having to ask the question. However, if there remained the smallest, most incremental chance he had not disappeared from her life as she suspected, she wanted to know. Had to know.

"Where is who?" Her sister's frown deepened. "Devil?"

Evie almost corrected her with *Theo* until she realized how her familiarity would appear. As if she had been intimate with him. As if she were in love with him. All of which she was, of course.

Good heavens.

She barely stifled a bitter bark of laughter.

"Yes," she managed. "Mr. Winter. Where has he gone?"

"I do not know where, only that he was called away." Addy shook her head. "Back to The Devil's Spawn, I expect, though Dom does his best to spare me from such matters. But it is you who must give me answers, Evie. Devil's letter was most distressing. If you were feeling so poorly, why did you not give us warning before now? Despite the danger, we would have found a way to help you."

The danger, yes.

Evie had all but forgotten about that in her distraction. A certain man had occupied her every thought these last two sennights. He occupied them still, in fact. She suspected he would never stop.

But he had left her.

He was gone.

He had stripped her of her garments, taken her to the heights of pleasure, and then, he had disappeared. She ought to have suspected he would, at the very least. But she was ever the naïve, hopeful duke's daughter he accused her of being. His fool, it would seem.

She was not going to allow him to disappear, however.

If he thought he could simply call back those walls that had come crumbling down between them in the early hours of the morning, he was wrong.

"Evie?"

Her sister's worried face hovered before her, tearing her from her tumultuous thoughts.

"I am not ill," she managed to say.

At least, not in the sense Addy had been led to believe by Theo's nonsensical missive and obvious attempts to force her from his life.

"Not ill?" Addy blinked. "I do not understand. Devil said it was imperative that I come to see you. He sent Blade here in his stead, to make certain you are protected."

Blade? Did every Winter sibling possess a dubious sobriquet?

She shook her head, dreadfully distressed by this sudden, unwanted development. "Theo was being dishonest with you, Addy. He wanted you here so I would not go chasing after him."

Yes, that was the only thing that made sense. He wanted to retreat to the East End, and he did not want her to follow. That was why he had taken her to his bed. Last night had been his farewell.

"Theo?" It was Addy's turn to look confused now.

Drat, she had forgotten herself after all.

A flush stole over her cheeks as she thought about the man she had come to know, quite different from the beast she had initially supposed him to be. His head between her thighs mere hours before, his tongue inside her.

"Mr. Winter," she managed to correct herself, plucking at

the coverlet in her agitation and avoiding her sister's knowing gaze. "His Christian name is Theodore."

"Good heavens, Devil told you his Christian name?"

"I was quite merciless until he did," she admitted, because there was no use in keeping the way she felt for Theo a secret from her twin.

She and Addy shared a unique bond, as close as two sisters could be. No one knew her better than Addy did. Except mayhap Theo, for she had shared parts of herself with him that she had never shared with anyone else.

"This is worse than you being ill, is it not?" Addy pressed, already sensing the truth.

She bit her lip, misery swamping her as she lifted her eyes to meet her twin's once more. "I am in love with Theo, Addy."

"Oh, darling. You are betrothed to Lord Denton." There was sympathy in her sister's countenance. Worry, too.

"I have discovered I no longer wish to become his wife."

"But Devil? Father will be furious, and I have no doubt he shall blame all this upon me." Addy's frown deepened. "In a sense, I suppose it is my fault. I never should have allowed the two of you to be here unchaperoned, in spite of the danger. But I never imagined… Devil scarcely speaks, and the two of you seemed enemies at first sight."

What Addy said was mostly true. Their father had nearly had an apoplectic fit when Addy had returned from Oxfordshire married to Mr. Dominic Winter, the illegitimate owner of one of London's most infamous gaming hells. Although Mr. Winter had proven himself an excellent husband to Addy—doting and loving in a fashion one never would have expected from the otherwise ruthless crime lord—their father still had not warmed to the notion of his daughter married to a commoner.

Evie's marriage to Denton was to have been the balm upon the wound. A means of removing the taint of scandal from the Duke of Linross's precious reputation. And Evie herself had not minded. Lord Denton was handsome, sought after, the perfect match in every way.

Save the only one she now realized mattered most.

She was not in love with him, and nor would she ever be.

Her heart belonged to one man alone.

"I cannot explain what happened," Evie admitted softly, slowly. "I did not care for him at first, it is true. I thought him a rude ogre of a man. But he is not at all the man I supposed him to be."

"I do not understand. If you are in love with Devil, why has he suddenly gone from your side? Why did he send me a note suggesting you were ill and that I needed to attend you immediately?" her twin asked.

"Because he believes we are too different, that our worlds cannot mingle. He is trying to keep me from him, to put distance between us and prove to me that a lady and a man born on the wrong side of the blanket cannot find happiness together."

That part still hurt her heart quite desperately. Knowing he would sooner disappear than fight for her… *Oh, Theo.* She would fight for them both. However she must. She vowed it.

"It would not be easy for you to be certain," Addy said. "There will be some doors that forever close to you, as they have for me. Our society can forgive many sins, but mesalliances are not one of them."

Evie knew that already, of course, as did Addy. From the time they had been old enough to walk, the rigid notion of propriety, the rules of society, and every expectation their parents had for them had been rigidly ingrained upon them. For all that, they had turned into quite the scandalous lot.

Their sister Hannah had been forced into a marriage of convenience by their father to hide her past indiscretions. She had been quite miserable and had only just reunited with the man she loved. Addy had married Dominic Winter, their brother Max was a notorious ne'er do well, and now Evie intended to jilt Lord Denton and chase after Theo.

Supposing he would have her, that was.

The reminder of his morning defection stung anew.

"I do not know if Theo wishes to marry me. Certainly, he has never spoken of such matters," she confessed. "I...have no expectations."

Not even after what had passed between them. He had taken care not to make love to her completely. Evie may have never kissed a man until Theo, but her insatiable curiosity, coupled with some salacious novels Addy had pilfered from their brother's belongings, meant she knew enough to understand what they had done together hours before had left her a virgin.

Because he intended for her to marry Lord Denton.

Her heart gave a pang.

"He said nothing to you?" her twin asked.

"Of course he did not." She sighed. "Theo is... He guards his heart well, I believe. But it is there, big and tender and generous. I want to be the one to keep it, to protect it, if only he will let me."

"Evie, please tell me you have not been...indecorous with my husband's brother," Addy said, her tone scandalized.

Evie bit her lip, pondering her sister's words. "Mayhap you ought to define indecorous. Your notion of it may differ from mine."

Addy's eyes widened. "You know quite well what I mean. Have you allowed him liberties?"

"Pray, do not act shocked, sister mine." Evie raised a

brow. "Have you forgotten it was I who helped you to sneak away to The Devil's Spawn without getting caught? Or that you returned at nearly dawn, looking as if you had been utterly debauched?"

Because Evie rather suspected her sister had been debauched that night, though Addy had remained somewhat secretive about what had transpired between herself and Mr. Winter at the time. Evie did not think the gentle roundness swelling behind her sister's gown could suggest anything other than a thorough bedding on the evening in question.

Addy flushed. "Of course I have not forgotten, but that was different, Evie. I was aiding Max."

"Max should never have involved you in his recklessness," Evie countered. "But that is neither here nor there. You cannot play the role of outraged sister with me. You are no stranger to scandal yourself. Goodness, none of us are."

Addy sighed. "I merely want to protect you, Evie. I fear I have already brought enough danger and upheaval into your life by marrying Dom. If it were not for me, you would never have been shot by brigands. And now, you are speaking of upending your entire future after a fortnight spent with a man whose acquaintance you have only recently made. A gentleman you were quite strong in professing your dislike for."

"Do not look at me as if I have lost my wits, Addy. I know what I want, and it is not to be Lady Denton. I want to follow my heart as you have done. I want a love like Romeo and Juliet's."

"Romeo and Juliet both ended up dead," Addy observed grimly.

"Not the conclusion of their love," Evie explained. "But the strength of it, the way it endured despite all the obstacles between them. The way they loved each other, though to the outside world it seemed they should not."

If only she knew Theo's true feelings for her. He had certainly never mentioned love. Neither had she, however.

"You are certain you are in love with Devil Winter?" her sister asked, searching her gaze.

"I have never been more certain of anything else. I cannot be Lord Denton's wife, Addy. Not when my heart belongs to another. It would not be fair to either one of us, and I cannot live the rest of my life longing for the one who could have made me whole. I do not care about the circumstances of his birth. Nor do I care for society or doors that may close to me. He is all I need and everything I want."

"I know the feeling, because it is the way I feel about my own husband." Addy covered Evie's hand with hers. "Love is stronger than fear. If you are in love with Devil, then you should tell him. See where he stands, and then decide what you shall do from there."

Relief and gratitude rushed over her, along with love for her twin. "Thank you, sister."

Her decision had been made. She was going to tell Theo she was in love with him.

All she had to do was find him first.

Chapter Ten

THE EAST END was always changing. Families came to power and then sank to the depths of poverty. Babes were born. Men and women died. Buildings were torn asunder or destroyed by flame, only to be replaced with new brick and mortar. New gaming hells opened with regularity. Enemies were always out to prosper. And most men did not possess a goddamn mite's worth of honor.

One thing that would never change: Devil Winter would do everything he could to protect his family. And that was why he was being ushered to the lair of one Jasper Sutton alone, with nary a weapon to defend himself. Sutton and his family had long been the nemesis of the Winter clan.

But at the moment, Devil needed the bastard's help.

They had a common enemy who, if what he had learned the night before was to be believed, was also behind the recent fires at The Devil's Spawn and the shots that had been fired at Evie. His need to protect her was stronger than his pride.

He would swallow every last drop he possessed—and poison too—if it meant keeping her safe.

Sutton was on his feet behind a desk fine enough to rival Dom's, carved lion heads adorning each of the four legs. He was a formidable man, with a height to rival Devil's and a similarly brutish size. But he also had a bloody reputation and a penchant for poaching Winter customers and staff. He had become a master at copying everything the Winters did. Prizefights, gaming, wenches at the green baize, hiring a French chef, discovering the source of all their smuggled Scots whisky…the list went on.

Their rivalry had quickly become bitter.

But now, another potential enemy, more dangerous and depraved, and far more willing to hurt anyone he could—even an innocent lady—was attempting to move in on their shared territory. The thought of the son of a whore made Devil's blood boil, the need to exact vengeance all-consuming.

"We meet again, Winter," Sutton drawled.

He was referring to their last, unexpectedly civil meeting at The Devil's Spawn when Sutton had conceded his waterworks to Devereaux Winter in exchange for one of Winter's prized warehouses near the docks. The bargain had won Dom the goodwill of his wife and had granted the Winters control over the quality and price of their water.

Devil offered a mocking bow, playing the part of civilized gentleman. "Thank you for agreeing to see me. Could've managed without a dozen of your lackeys searching me for guns and shivs."

Sutton inclined his head. "An eye for an eye, a twat for a twat."

Christ, but this man nettled him. "Tooth for a tooth, Sutton."

Sutton clasped his hands behind his back and strolled forward. "Nay. 'Tis a twat for a twat in this instance. Your brother came to me for a set of petticoats and now you. Besides. You're both twats."

Devil stiffened. What could Jasper Sutton know of Evie? His hands clenched into fists at his sides. "Watch your tongue, Sutton, else I may be tempted to rip it out and feed it to one of your bloody mongrels."

Jasper Sutton's hounds were menacing and notoriously vicious. Word had it they had torn many a trespasser or a thief's limbs from his body.

"My dogs only have a taste for the blood of my enemies," Sutton said. "You'd make a feast for them."

"I did not come here to wage war with you, Sutton," he gritted.

"Fuck." Sutton whistled. "Always carrying the keg, Devil Winter. Never could take a goddamn joke. If I wanted my dogs to eat you, you'd already be dead."

Hardly comforting, as reassurances went.

Devil ground his molars and chose to ignore his foe's taunts. "You have had fires in your hell recently. Fancy nibs getting fleeced in the street when they leave, aye? The charleys have been paid off, and one of your shipments of whisky was stolen."

Sutton's eyes narrowed. "The work of Winters, surely."

"Not after we have given our word," Devil countered. "We have our honor."

"And a whole lot of different whores for mothers."

Devil shrugged. Insults to the woman who had birthed him affected him not. "Mayhap. No different for Suttons, is it?"

The Sutton family was larger than the Winters. More brutal. Their lineage questionable at best.

"Take care. Won't be good for me to get crabbed." Sutton's lip curled. "You'll get no help from me if you can't be civil, Winter."

Devil raised a brow. "I respond in kind. An eye for an eye and a twat for a twat, isn't it?"

Jasper Sutton appeared distinctly unimpressed by his attempt at a joke, even after he had just insulted Devil's ability to take one. "You're a bold one, sauntering into my territory, needing my help. Thought you said you had a square thing for me."

"I do, but first, I need your promise that you will help me."

Sutton nodded. "I promise."

"Not good enough." Devil knew Jasper Sutton. They had been battling for far too long. The man's word was worth less than a bob. "I need proof."

"Fuck." Sutton's eyes narrowed once more. "Fine. I'll return the little shite what's been haunting my alleys and filching all the coin and watches from the pockets of every nib who leaves my hell. He says he belongs to you Winters anyway. Glad to get him off my hands."

Surprised filtered through Devil. "Davy?"

He hadn't had an inkling that the troublesome young pickpocket his brother had taken in and brought to The Devil's Spawn had been missing. But then, he supposed the time he had spent with Evie had isolated him from his world and his family more than he had realized. Almost a fortnight, and it had changed every bloody thing.

"Aye, that's the scamp's name. A slippery one, that. Tipped us the Dublin packet many a night until we caught him. You can have him back if you promise to keep him where he belongs."

Hell.

Of course, Dom would want the little bugger back. He was an honorary Winter now, despite the reckless hellion's rebellious nature. His brother was overtly fond of Davy, but then, he was also soft as a pie since he'd gone and fallen in love with Lady Adele.

Then again, Devil could not blame him. He was similarly soft over Lady Evie.

"I will take the lad with me," Devil allowed. "And I will

accept your promise of his return as proof enough. What do you know of Paul Wilmore?"

Once more, Sutton sneered. "That he is a son of a whore and ought to be beaten to death with a sack of his own shit."

Well. That was certainly...honesty. Devil could work with that.

"What if I were to tell you I know far more about him? That he is the man who is behind not only the fires at your hell but The Devil's Spawn as well, and that he has been paying men to cheat at our hells, steal from our patrons, and shoot at innocent ladies?"

"I would tell you no lady is innocent," Sutton said, his countenance guarded. "But then I would also tell you I want to know more. And I want evidence that what you say is true."

"I have one of his men," Devil said. "He will tell the tale better than I can, if you will but see him."

After he had returned Evie to her chamber that morning, he had been restless, unable to sleep. Despite the fact he had managed no slumber at all, his body had reached the point where his lack of rest no longer mattered. When he had discovered the truth about Paul Wilmore the night before, he had been elated. And then, when he had comprehended the full extent of the sins the bastard had committed, he had been outraged. His fury had taken him to the matches Wilmore held.

His opponent had been no match for Devil's fury. He had beaten him to the point of unconsciousness, and then he had made certain he had learned everything there was to know about Wilmore. Including the efforts he had recently been taking to undermine both the Winters and the Suttons. Devil had dragged the bastard back to The Devil's Spawn himself, where he had been under guard until bringing the man to Jasper Sutton so he could play the bird and sing.

Like a man possessed, Devil had returned to the townhome expecting to formulate his strategy. Instead, Evie had been awaiting him. But after her desires had been slaked, there had been no sleep for Devil. No rest. There had only been the burning urge to do what he must. To sever ties with Evie and see that Wilmore got what he deserved, whilst leaving Evie forever safe.

As safe as she could be.

But time and distance from Dom, Devil, and the rest of the East End Winters would give her that. Especially after she became Lady Denton.

At the notion, he bit his lip so hard, the metallic tang of blood invaded his mouth. Christ, he had wounded himself.

At long last, Jasper Sutton gave a short, jerky nod of approval. "Bring him to me."

It was only then Devil realized he had been holding his breath.

He inhaled, the rush of air making his lungs burn. It was the most he had felt since leaving Evie for good earlier that morning.

Chapter Eleven

IN THE END, Evie wrote Lord Denton a letter, crying off.

It was not the manner in which she had intended to deliver the news of her change of heart. However, Addy was adamant that it remained unsafe for Evie to traipse about London. Seeking Denton out was impossible and scandalous, and as he believed her rusticating in the countryside in aid to her mother and grandmother, her sudden reappearance would spark confusion and, with it, the resulting wagging of tongues.

Addy had proven the voice of reason, urging Evie to accept Blade Winter's protection and traveling with him to The Devil's Spawn. In veils, of course. No one must recognize her once she arrived, were she to be observed by any of the lords who patronized Addy's husband's establishment.

And so it was that she found herself being transported to a gaming hell in the East End in the midst of the day, accompanied by a man named after a weapon.

Blade Winter was quiet, seated opposite her, idly toying with a dagger that appeared terrifically sharp. And yet, he ran his thumb over its edge as if it could do him no harm.

"Is Blade your true Christian name?" she asked at last, curious, and also seeking some distraction.

Her heart and mind were at war. And she was terrified Theo would reject her. That he would once more push her away as thoroughly as he had on nearly every occasion they had been alone. Every occasion save last night, of course. The reminder made her belly clench and heat slide between her thighs. Her cheeks also went hot.

She shifted on her seat, attempting to get comfortable.

Blade stroked the pad of his thumb over the fearsome point of his dagger, eying her. "Why do you ask?"

"Devil's true name is Theodore. It stands to reason that your name is not Blade," she said.

Blade stilled, then cried out. Scarlet dripped form his thumb, running down his wicked-looking dagger. He must have pressed too hard upon the point. Mayhap distracted by her question. He held the wounded flesh to his lips and sucked. But it was too late. Blood had already dripped down his wrist, staining his shirtsleeves, and fallen upon his breeches, marring the otherwise faultless fabric.

"Oh dear." Evie pulled a handkerchief from her reticule and offered it to him. "Here you are, sir. This ought to stem the flow."

"I'll mark it with my blood, my lady," he pointed out.

Did he truly fear she would mind? *Good heavens*, the man had cut himself because of her, and all she wanted was to stop the bleeding.

"I do not care if the handkerchief is ruined," she assured him. "Tend to yourself, please."

He wrapped it tightly about his thumb and then pinned her with a searching gaze. Like Theo, Blade's stare was bright, striking, and blue. He, too, was a handsome man. But he was golden haired to Theo's dark, masculine beauty. She could see they shared a father rather than a mother—their frames, all broad shoulders and sinuous muscle, were the same.

"Devil's name is Theodore?" he asked at length.

Did he not know?

Could it be possible Theo had shared a secret with her that he had never allowed another to know? Not even his own brother?

Evie tried to quell the hope rising within her—foolish and futile at this juncture—and failed, nonetheless.

"Of course it is," she said calmly, impressing herself with her lack of emotion. "Surely he must have told you, Mr. Blade?"

He grinned, as if she had just said something amusing. "No mister. Blade will do. And no, Lady Evangeline, my brother Devil has never told me his Christian name is Theodore. I can understand why."

She frowned at him. "Why?"

"Theodore is a soft name. Would hardly strike fear into the hearts of enemies." Blade Winter chuckled.

"He is not as ferocious as he seems. Theo suits him far more than Devil does."

He gave her a strange look, one she could not decipher. "You seem quite familiar with Devil."

Her cheeks went hot as she recalled just how familiar she was. But she would not look away. If she was to be a part of Theo's world, she would have to familiarize herself with it. There was no room for shame or propriety and rules.

"If I am?" she asked Blade.

He studied her for far longer than she would have preferred, until her ears went hot beneath the force of his scrutiny. At long last, he nodded, as if he had reached a decision of some sort. "Aye. You'll do."

She would do?

What did that mean?

Before she could ask either question, their carriage rocked to a halt. "We've arrived, my lady. Flip down your veil and do not stray from my side."

She did as he directed. "Thank you for bringing me here, Blade. I cannot tell you how much I appreciate your kindness."

"I ain't kind, Lady Evangeline," her escort bit out. "But I love my brother and if you're his woman, then you're family to me."

Her heart swelled at his words—and at the notion, utterly wondrous—of being Theo's woman. But before she could respond, the door to the carriage opened abruptly. Dom Winter stood there with a troubled countenance, a young boy with an impossibly dirty face at his side.

"I need you, Blade," he said curtly without acknowledging Evie's presence.

She had shielded her face, it was true, but he knew Blade had been acting as her bodyguard in Theo's stead. This was a side of her brother-in-law she had never seen, and it filled her with misgiving, tying her stomach in knots. Mr. Winter had always been gentlemanly and considerate in her presence, charming and sweet with Addy. A worried Dominic Winter could only be a harbinger of something bad.

Something—mayhap—that related to Theo. *Dear God.*

Blade exited the carriage, his entire bearing changing. An ominous intensity poured from him and if he had not just traveled with her from Mayfair, civilized and polite as can be—aside from his dagger and the blood, of course—she would have sworn him a different man altogether. The misgiving within her blossomed and grew, flooding her.

"What is it?" Blade bit out.

Evie clambered out of the carriage as well, desperate for answers.

Mr. Winter offered her an abbreviated bow. "My lady. Forgive me, but there is a matter of grave import my brother and I must attend. Davy will show you inside to a private salon where you can make yourself comfortable."

"You need not go to trouble on my behalf," she said, hoping to garner some answers. To find Theo. "I only wish to speak to Theo."

Her brother-in-law's brow furrowed. "Theo?"

"Devil, apparently," Blade said, raising a sardonic brow.

Mr. Winter muttered an epithet. "God willing, he shall speak with you soon enough. However, for the moment, I must insist you go with Davy."

Something was wrong, Evie knew it.

"I am not going anywhere until you tell me what is happening," she countered. "If Theo is in danger—"

"He is," her brother-in-law interrupted. "And that is why you must go with Davy. Blade and I will do everything we can to help him. But for now, what he needs more than anything is for you to remain safe."

A gasp tore from her, fear clawing her from within. "What is happening? Where is he?"

"Go with Davy," her brother-in-law told her, his tone sharp enough for her to know he, too, feared whatever situation Theo had found himself in. "Devil will wish to know you are unharmed. Blade and I will do everything we can to bring him back to you."

She swallowed, looking to the lad with the soiled face. He grinned, offering her his arm. "This way, m'lady."

She glanced back at Addy's husband, whose expression was grave.

"Trust me, Lady Evie. He is our brother, and we will do everything we can to bring him back to you. But time is wasting, and we must go."

Of course. The bond between all the Winter siblings was incredibly strong. She knew that from Addy. And she knew it from Theo himself. Whatever the situation in which Theo had suddenly found himself embroiled, she had to trust her brother-in-law.

"Go to him, then," she managed, barely avoiding bursting into fearful tears. The tremor in her voice said enough.

She took the filthy urchin's proffered arm and allowed herself to be led into The Devil's Spawn.

THE PLAN HAD been simple.

But like all simple plans, it quickly become complicated. And then, it became downright deadly.

The barrel of a pistol in his lower back told Devil he'd found Paul Wilmore in the instant before the bastard's growl was in his ear.

"Fine day to die, Winter."

Icy dread slid through him.

Fucking hell.

This was not the way he had intended to cross paths with Wilmore. The bastard was supposed to have been within his private rooms, bedding one of his harlots. Obviously that bit of information had been wrong.

"Wilmore," he bit out. "Coward's way, is it?"

"Smart way, the way I sees it. End an enemy before 'e ends me."

"I didn't come here to kill you," he gritted. Not entirely true. "If I wanted you dead, I'd have sent Blade to do the job, and you'd be bleeding on the floor as we speak."

Also not complete truth. Blade was no stranger to killing. However, Devil wanted to be the one to defend Evie. To make certain she was safe. He had to do that for her, because he could never have her for himself.

"You'll pardon me for not believin' a word you say, Winter," Wilmore spat.

Devil did not blame him. Wilmore was no fool, even if he was reckless and ruthless. Else he would not have been capable of scraping and clawing his way up in the East End to where he was now, flush enough with power that he dared to torment the two most powerful families in the rookeries.

Devil inclined his head, aware his position was precarious at best. Jasper Sutton was no solid ally, and although he had promised the aid of his men, Devil did not entirely trust him. And whilst he had sent Davy back to The Devil's Spawn with an order to tell Blade and Dom what was unfolding, he was not certain the rascal would not find another tempting pocket to pick on his way home. Devil ought to have gone back to the hell himself to fetch his brothers, but Sutton had wanted to move on Wilmore immediately and Devil had not wanted his sometime nemesis to allow Wilmore to tip them the Dublin packet.

"You don't have to believe me, Wilmore," he said calmly now, taking care to remain immobile as his mind whirled and madly plotted a means of saving himself. "But I would appreciate it if you hear me speak before putting a ball in my back."

"Less trouble to kill you now," Wilmore returned.

Also an excellent point, but Devil wasn't about to admit that.

"If you kill me, the Winters will have their vengeance," he tried next, for this, too, was truth. His siblings were loyal. They were family. They were all they had. And they would—every last one of them, from Dom to Gen and Gavin or Demon and Blade—give up their lives to save one another. "There will be nowhere for you to hide that they will not find you and destroy you. Is that what you want, Wilmore? Dead men can't get rich."

The man's pause was telling.

He was contemplating Devil's words. Weighing his choic-es.

"What the fuck are you doin' in my 'ell?" Wilmore spat.

"What the fuck were you doing having your men shoot at my brother's sister-in-law?" he countered.

How odd it seemed to refer to Evie in such bland terms. As if she had no relation to him, as if he scarcely knew her. When, in truth, he knew her. He knew her lips beneath his, her sweet curves, her scent, her taste, how to make her come undone.

He bit his already abused lower lip hard enough to draw forth more blood. An excellent distraction. He could not afford to be weak in this moment. He had to be strong and firm, to deflect and defend.

"Sister-in-law?" Wilmore asked then.

"Lady Evangeline Saltisford," he elaborated. "Daughter to the Duke of Linross. One of your lackeys shot at her once, nearly wounding Viscount Denton. And on the second try, he shot Lady Evangeline herself."

"Fuck."

Wilmore's low curse said more than any other response could have.

Understanding dawned on Devil. "You never intended anyone to be shot, did you? I am going to step away from your weapon and turn to face you at the count of five."

"You can count to five, can you?" Wilmore taunted. "Thought you was a simpleton."

Devil clenched his jaw, doing his best to ignore the old hurts. "Aye. I can count."

He barely refrained from adding *you worthless arsehole* to his response.

And then, he did as he had warned. What else had he to

lose? He had already lost Evie. There was precious little left. He moved, holding his breath as he went, at any moment expecting to feel the blast of Wilmore's gun lodging in his head or spine.

Instead, he spun, facing Wilmore and an ominous double-barrel flintlock.

Still, he was not dead. There was that.

"Stay where you are, Winter," the other man warned.

Devil had no doubt Wilmore would shoot him dead without a hint of conscience. However, he also knew men of Wilmore's ilk. The bastard was likely fretting over Devil's words, wondering what would befall him if he dared to kill a Winter. His concern for his own worthless hide was trumping all else.

"Consider what will happen to you if I am injured," he reminded his opponent. "Or worse."

"Not sure I give a damn about what will happen either way," Wilmore sneered.

A flash of movement caught Devil's attention then. *By God*, he had never been more relieved to see Jasper Sutton. Presuming Sutton would aid him, that was. Hoping Wilmore had not taken note of Devil's traveling gaze, he jerked his stare back to the man with the gun pointed at his heart.

"You will give a damn when my brother is slitting your throat," he told Wilmore smoothly.

Meanwhile, Sutton took his position behind Wilmore, raising his own weapon.

"Eh. Might be worth killing you to bring old Dom Winter out of 'iding. Married a fancy duke's daughter and thinks 'imself too good for the rookeries, does 'e?" Wilmore taunted. "Mayhap spilling your worthless blood will get 'is attention."

"What is it you hope to gain?" he asked, attempting to

drag out the moment, give Sutton enough time to act.

Wilmore grinned. "Power. Coin. What does anyone want? I've had enough chatter, Winter. What did you come 'ere for?"

Vengeance.

To make certain no harm would ever come to Evie again.

"To speak with you," he said, and that was not entirely a falsehood.

"Not in the mood." Wilmore cocked his head. "Get ready to cock up your toes—"

A feral cry interrupted Wilmore's words, stealing his attention. He jerked.

Everything unfolded in a hazy blur. Shots rang out. A blazing pain seared through Devil's shoulder. He reached for his own hidden weapon, but in the next moment, he took a vicious blow to the head. Everything went black.

His last thoughts were of Evie as he fell into the void.

Chapter Twelve

A TRAY OF tea had been delivered, but Evie had not been able to stomach a sip. She was a massive knot of worry mingled with fear. The Winters had yet to return, and the scamp who was doing his utmost to entertain her was not distraction enough to serve as a balm for her frayed nerves.

She paced the salon for what must have been the hundredth time—a habit she was engaging in with alarming frequency of late—and turned back to discover her reticule gone. Her gaze traveled to the urchin, whose face was still quite streaked with dirt, and who was in the midst of regaling her with a tale of a litter of kittens he had recently rescued from the streets.

"Ashes, she's the sweetest one of them all, milady. Gray with green eyes."

"Davy?" She moved toward him, brows raised.

"Aye, milady?" He gave her a gap-toothed grin she suspected had gotten him out of any number of scrapes. "Want a kitten, do you? His nabs don't want me to keep them all. Says we'll be overrun if I do. Says I needs to find homes. I can go and fetch Ashes for you, if you like."

He was attempting to distract her, but she was not fooled in the least.

She reached him and held out her hand. "Where is my reticule?"

He blinked. "Rettycule?"

"Shall I empty all your pockets? Or perhaps when Mr. Winter returns he can hold you upside down and see if my belongings fall out."

Naughty lad, thinking he could thieve her reticule without her realizing it. She was distressed, but she still had eyes, and her reticule had been on the settee where she had left it one moment and gone the next.

The boy's smile faded. "Don't tell his nabs. I ain't supposed to be filching here."

"Return my reticule, and he shall be none the wiser," she allowed grimly.

The little rogue plucked it from his coat and returned it to her with a grumble.

"Thank you." She looked inside to make certain he had not removed anything.

But in the next moment, she forgot all about her reticule. A great commotion had risen in the hall beyond the salon.

"Where is she?"

She recognized that roar.

Evie's hand flew to her heart and she raced toward the door. It flew open to reveal a bloodied, pale Theo. There was scarlet on his face, staining his white shirtsleeves. So much blood. And this time, there was also a wound evident beneath the tattered remnants of his garment.

Dear God, he had been shot.

"Theo!" she cried out, rushing to him. "What has happened? I was so worried."

"What the hell are you doing here, Lady Evangeline?" he demanded, his voice cold and harsh, bearing the lash of a whip.

His countenance was ashen, but his blue eyes held the chill of ice. He appeared furious with her. And he had called her Lady Evangeline.

Not Evie.

Not even milady.

But Lady Evangeline.

"I..." She faltered, taken aback by his appearance and his reaction. "I came here to see you."

Dom and Blade Winter appeared behind him, Dom settling a hand on Theo's uninjured shoulder. "Come, Devil. You've lost enough blood as it is. You need to see the doctor."

"Fuck the doctor," he growled, his gaze never straying from Evie's. "I want her gone."

The tender lover of the night before had vanished. In his place was a feral, angry creature. What had she done to warrant such a reaction from him? Where had he gone? And what had happened to him?

"Theo," she said, reaching for him. "What is happening? How badly are you hurt?"

His lip curled. "I'll survive. Go back to Mayfair where you belong."

"Not until you speak with me." She shook her head. "I am not going anywhere with you wounded and bleeding. Your brother is right. You need to see a doctor at once."

He swayed but caught himself and did not fall.

He was badly wounded.

"You need to leave," he told her, his voice as cutting as a dagger.

"I will not leave when you need me." How did he think she could go when he was grievously injured, bleeding and unsteady on his feet? Her heart could not withstand any more worry and fear this day. She could not stray from his side. No matter how biting and angry the words he directed at her.

"I don't need you." He swayed again. "I never did. Get the hell out of here. You have nothing to fear any longer. The man responsible for the danger surrounding you is dead."

"Come, brother," Dom urged him again. "You are bleeding all over the goddamn carpet."

So he was. Evie gasped as she realized blood was running down Theo's arm, dripping off his limp hand, pooling on the floor.

"Go home, duke's daughter," Theo snarled at her. "You do not belong here."

He listed once more, and then he went paler, his eyes rolling back in his head. He collapsed against Dom and Blade, who caught his large frame with ease.

Fear washed over her, making her mouth go dry. She rushed forward, uncertain of what she could do for him, if anything. Needing to touch him, to be reassured he was still breathing. She swiped a lock of hair from his brow, absorbing the warmth of his skin.

"He needs surgery," Dom told her gently, but his expression was strained. "He has lost a great deal of blood, and we haven't any time to waste."

"Of course." She nodded, swallowing against a rush of bile. "Do what you must. I shall wait here."

With that, Dom and Blade hauled an unconscious Theo from the salon.

Taking her heart with them.

THE WAIT WAS excruciating.

Addy had arrived to keep Evie company, but not even the presence of her twin could diminish the fear and worry churning within her.

"You must try to calm yourself, dearest," Addy reminded her now, her voice tender but firm. "I am certain all will be well."

She wished she possessed her sister's aptitude for thinking the best in a wretched situation. Addy was a ray of sunlight; she saw the goodness in everyone and everything. In the current moment, Evie was a storm cloud.

"I cannot be calm," she told Addy. "Will you check and see if Dom has any word yet?"

"Darling, he promised he would come to us as soon as the surgeon has finished." Addy put a comforting arm around Evie's shoulders. "Shall I ring for some tea? Have you eaten anything today?"

"I cannot eat." Hunger had become obsolete. All she wanted was to know about Theo, how he had fared.

If he would live.

Dear God, he had to live.

She could not bear to think of him dying, and all because he had been so intent upon saving her.

"Just some biscuits, perhaps," Addy tried.

"This is all my fault," Evie said, closing her eyes against a fresh rush of tears. "If it were not for me, he would not have been wounded."

"You must not blame yourself for what happened," her twin told her, still remaining the calm Evie needed. "What is most important is that the man behind the attacks on you cannot hurt you any longer. Nor can he hurt any of us. Devil will be well, I am certain."

"I wish I possessed your certainty," she said bitterly. "I am terrified, Addy."

"Nothing is certain, of course," Addy said, giving her shoulders another squeeze of sisterly solidarity. "However, all we have is hope and faith. We must trust in both."

Her sister was too good.

Too sweet.

And Evie was all too fallible.

She was about to respond in kind when the door opened and Dom Winter appeared on the threshold once more, looking weary and grim.

Her heart fell to her slippers as she leapt to her feet. "How is he?"

"The surgeon is finished with his work. It went well, he believes, and fortunately the ball passed through in a clean fashion, avoiding bone or muscle. If he does not suffer an infection, the surgeon is confident he will maintain the use of his arm."

Relief hit her. "Thank heavens. Where is he? I must go to him."

"Forgive me," her brother-in-law said softly, his countenance softening with sympathy. "But he does not want to see you."

"Surely not. That cannot be." She searched Dom's dark gaze. "I know what he said before, but he did not mean it, I am certain."

"He is adamant." Dom paused then, raking his fingers through his hair in a gesture that suggested he was not as calm as he outwardly seemed. "In his state, I think it best not to cause him any further upset. He has asked that you return home."

"Without seeing him?" The despair she had been barely keeping at bay for hours returned, fiercer than ever. "Without speaking with him?"

"It is what Devil wishes," her brother-in-law said.

She closed her eyes for a moment, feeling dizzy. The combination of the extreme emotions she had experienced over the last few hours along with her refusal to take sustenance was finally having an effect upon her.

Theo did not want her here.

He was pushing her away, resurrecting all the walls keeping them apart once more. Why? Did he truly believe she could not be happy sharing her life with him? Did he fear the potential for danger? Or was it merely a more painful truth—that he was not in love with her?

A strong hand steadied her. But it was not the hand she wanted.

"Lady Evie?" Dom's voice prodded. "Are you well? You look pale."

Inhaling slowly, she opened her eyes, hating the pity she saw reflected on her brother-in-law's face. "I am as well as I can be. Will you...will you tell Theo I wish him well?"

Her voice broke on the last word, as the possible finality of this moment hit her. Theo had not died today, but he intended to disappear from her life just the same.

For now, she had no choice but to let him.

Chapter Thirteen

THE PAIN WAS scorching. Searing. Intense.

He was dwelling in some manner of hell. That had to be the answer for it. He was hot. Aflame. Burning alive. Devil had never known such agony, such acute misery.

But through it all, there was something, a presence, a lightness. And somehow, he knew that presence was her.

Evie.

He tried to say her name, but all he managed was a croak.

A soft, soothing voice reached him. A cool cloth bathed his brow.

And then he surrendered to the darkness once more.

HE WAS DROWNING in a sea. Struggling to stay afloat, to paddle to the distant shore. But his shoulder was weak and painful. His left arm hung limply. Would he ever be able to use it again?

The mocking laughter echoed all around him.

He recognized the sound of that bitter cackle, that voice. The scent. Blue ruin.

The woman who had given him life had always stunk of it.

By the end, it had stolen her looks and robbed her of life.

Her eyes had been dull and lifeless, cold as her heart when he had seen her shortly before her death. She had come to ask him for coin, of all things. And Devil, stupid sod that he was, had given her some. Enough to keep food in her belly, to give her a roof over her head. But instead of spending it on such worthy necessities, she had used it to procure more spirits. The last penny he had ever given her had been poured down her throat.

"Stupid," she whispered, the taunt turning into a chant. "Stupid, stupid, stupid."

The dream shifted, changed.

He was no longer in the sea but at The Devil's Spawn.

Cora was there. Beautiful, faithless Cora.

Telling him he was not worthy of her. That she would sooner be a lord's whore than a thief's wife.

Her back was to him, and when he reached for her, she turned.

It was not Cora looking at him, but Evie.

Evie with her tousled golden curls and her tearstained face.

"Live for me," she whispered. "I love you."

"Evie," he tried to say, but his voice was hoarse.

She fell away.

That was when the flames returned, burning him into nothing.

DEVIL WOKE IN the night with a jolt, pain lancing him. His head ached. His shoulder was on fire. But hovering on the air was a sweet scent he recognized. Or at least, he thought he did.

That scent tore him from the bowels of whatever perdition he had been inhabiting. It called to him like a siren's song. He was in the grips of delirium again, he was sure. Delusional from the fevers attacking his body. Infection had set in, and he had been paying the price, torn between the abyss of mindlessness and terrible nightmares that threatened to steal his soul.

He was cloaked in darkness, the chamber bathed in shadows. He could scarcely keep his eyes open—the lids were so damn heavy. Nothing made sense, and yet everything did.

He recalled pieces of what had happened. Wilmore's pistol against his back, the gunfire that had erupted as Jasper Sutton had struck first, killing their mutual enemy.

Not before Wilmore had landed a bullet in Devil's shoulder, however.

None of that mattered. All that did matter was that Evie was safe. Wilmore's power had been doused by his death, and his men would be left scrambling. The hell would close. The threat was over.

And Devil had made certain she would return to her aristocratic world where she belonged. To the lord she would marry. The thought was more painful than the ball that had torn through his flesh.

He shifted on the bed, trying to find comfort for his aching back, but the movement was nigh impossible. His body felt as weak as a newborn foal's.

"Theo?"

The hopeful whisper was familiar.

Hers.

He inhaled sharply, but even that movement brought him pain. He clenched his jaw to stave off a wave of nausea.

Damn it, he had not been wrong about the scent. She was here, somewhere near to him in the darkness. He wanted to touch her so badly he shuddered. But then, he realized his teeth were chattering. And suddenly he was cold, so cold. Shaking with the chill. He could not get warm enough.

Nor could he speak.

Fingers gently stroked his hair. Soft, knowing, delicate fingers. He closed his eyes and thought of them, pale and elegant, the nails rounded, the pads silken. But she must not be here. Did she not understand? He was doing this for her. Because he could not bear for her to ever be in danger again. Because he could not make her his knowing she would one day resent him.

It was better this way.

She was too good for his sorry arse.

Better off without him.

She would see, one day.

But for now, he could not muster the desire to send her away. Not when she was touching him with such tenderness. He could almost pretend she loved him. Stupid, he knew.

No one could ever love Devil Winter.

Still, he closed his eyes and sank back into the alluring depths of sleep as her fingers gently swept over him.

MORNING DAWNED OVER the East End just as it did in Mayfair. The East End was louder, brasher, dirtier, more crowded and dangerous. Smellier, too. But the sun rose all the same.

Evie had pulled back the window dressings herself to allow light to filter into Theo's sickroom. She had also opened the window, and the evidence of the East End's sometimes pungent presence was making itself known as a swift breeze blew through the room. He needed sunlight. And fresh air. Unfortunately, the air was not terribly fresh. But it was better than the stale air of his sickroom, and it would have to do.

Evie bathed Theo's feverish forehead with a damp, cool cloth.

For days, she had stayed away, following his wishes. Until at last, Dom had told her Theo's condition had taken a grave turn. Infection had settled in. She had gone to The Devil's Spawn, determined that no one would get in the way of her seeing him and tending to him.

She had never felt more helpless in her life than she had when she had first entered his chamber to find him lying so pale and still upon his bed, his dark hair soaked with perspiration, the bandage on his shoulder soaked through with the balm she had applied and streaks of blood. The felled beast.

And she was responsible for everything that had happened to him.

That had been two days ago.

She had not left his side since, and she was determined she would not. Not until he opened his eyes and demanded she go. Or not until he breathed his last. She was more determined never to allow the latter to occur, to do everything in her power to see him live.

The horrible reality was that it was possible Theo would not survive the infection that had claimed him. That he would succumb to the fevers ravaging his body. A sob rose in her throat, but she forced it down, refusing to allow herself to cry. She had wept enough during the days she had honored his request for separation.

His skin felt cooler today than it had the day before, and she had sworn in the depths of the night that he had been awake. He had been moving, not thrashing in his bed as he did when in the grips of his delirium. But rather, his motions had seemingly been deliberate and slow. The actions of a lucid man.

At least, that was what she dared to hope.

She had stroked his hair until at last, his steady, reassuring breathing had lulled her into a brief, dreamless sleep. When the first strains of dawn had filtered through the curtains, she had been awake, checking him for any signs of change.

Praying and tending and loving—that was all she could do for him, and she was willing to perform them all, in any order, repeatedly, until he was well.

He shifted beneath her ministrations, a groan tearing from him, along with a hiss of pain as he attempted to move his injured shoulder.

Hope soared. "Theo?"

Long, dark lashes moved on his pale cheeks. Slowly, they rose, revealing his beloved blue gaze. Bluer than the summer sky in the country. Bluer than blue. And clear, lucid. No trace of fever in their depths.

"Why?" he rasped, attempting to say more but then stopping, running his tongue over his lower lip, which was cracked and dry.

"Water?" she asked.

He gave a jerky nod, and she rose with haste to fetch him some, bringing it back to the bedside and helping him to lift his head so he could take a proper drink. She allowed him three gulps before withdrawing the cup, not wishing for him to be ill after so many days of precious little water, and nothing but dribbles of broth spooned down his throat. He was weak and ill, and he needed to proceed slowly, as any invalid would.

"Why are you here?" he growled.

"How are you feeling?" she asked, ignoring his question.

"Why are you here?" he demanded once more.

Did she dare tell him the truth? That she was here because

she loved him? She did not think the weary, broken stranger glaring at her wanted to hear those words now. Mayhap not ever.

She needed to tread with care. "I am here because it is my fault you were wounded. It is my fault you suffered the infection and were so gravely ill these last few days."

"I told you to go."

His curt, cold voice did nothing to stay the hope and relief welling within her. He had not been this lucid since her arrival. And though he looked weak and pale—understandably after all the trauma he had just endured—there was a vitality about him which had been previously absent.

"Yes," she agreed calmly. "You did."

His eyes narrowed. "Don't want you here."

"So you have said repeatedly." Once more, she kept her tone bright, nary a hint of the hurt blossoming within her showing.

"Get out."

It was not the first time Theodore Winter had ordered her from his chamber; different room, different day. But Evie was not heeding him this time. She had before, and she had almost lost him. She was not about to lose him now.

"No."

His lip curled. "I don't want you here."

"Nevertheless, I am here. Remaining." She held the cup to his lips. "More water?"

He lifted his right hand and swatted the cup away, spilling its contents all over his counterpane and sloshing on her bodice in the process. It was terribly childish of him. And part of her she dared not reveal—the part of her that loved him desperately and had been terrified he would die all whilst she had been getting scarcely any rest—longed to cry. To run from the chamber and hide from his wrath.

But she reminded herself he was only trying to do what was best. The Theo Winter she had come to know was not a beast but a man. A good, kind man. A handsome, wonderful man. The man she loved.

"You have spilled the water all over your bedclothes," she observed calmly. "All you needed to do was say you were not thirsty, Theo. No need for theatrics."

"Devil," he gritted.

"You shall always be Theo to me," she told him pointedly, holding his gaze and daring him to defy her. To offer argument.

"Go," he ordered her again.

"As we have already established, I am not leaving." And damn him for waking from days of fever—for being at the edge of life and death—and then demanding she remove herself from his presence the instant he was awake. Part of her longed to box his ears. But another part of her longed to kiss him. She was so relieved he was awake and himself.

Surely this meant he was going to survive this.

"You do not belong here."

"I belong wherever you are." The impassioned words fled her before she could think better of them.

She had revealed too much. Made herself far too vulnerable.

He stared, his jaw rigid. "You don't belong with me, milady. I'm too stupid, an East End bastard born of a whore. Can't even read."

She flinched at his description of himself, but forged onward, needing him to see the difference. To see himself for the man he was instead of as the worthless boy his mother had taught him to believe he was. "Of course you can read. You have been making great progress, and you are not stupid at all,

Theo. Your brain sees the letters in a different order at times, and I believe that is what has caused you difficulty in the past."

He sneered. "Made you come and it's fogged your mind."

His crude words made her flush. "Do not make a mockery of yourself or what we shared, I beg you."

He stared at her, and she had to once more stifle the urge to weep. This was a different sort of misery altogether. "I've a lame arm."

Her gaze flicked to his wounded arm. She had seen him move it in the depths of his fevers, so she knew it was possible. Not to mention what the surgeon had told Dom. "Your brother said the surgeon was confident you should not lose any movement. The ball passed through, avoiding muscle and bone."

"Don't give a goddamn what the leech said. I know how my arm feels. Dead." As if to punctuate his words, he attempted to move the arm in question and then stopped, inhaling sharply, his expression clouding with pain.

"Stop, Theo," she said. "You will injure yourself further."

"Who bloody well cares?"

"I do!" She pressed a shaking hand over her heart, trying not to allow him to see how badly she was trembling just now. "I care, Theo."

But he remained impervious. "Go, milady. You aren't wanted or needed here."

He was breaking her heart, but she refused to allow him to see it. "You risked your life to see me safe. The least I can do is show you my appreciation."

"Don't want gratitude or pity from you."

Anger rose within her swiftly, usurping the pain for a heartbeat. "Then what is it you want from me?"

"For you to leave me alone. Marry Dullerton. Give him

half a dozen brats."

"Theo," she began, intending to tell him she had ended her betrothal to Lord Denton.

But he interrupted her by taking up the spilled cup in his right fist and hurling it to the wall behind her. It shattered into hundreds of pieces, raining to the floor.

"Get out," he roared.

She flinched, rising from the chair she had been occupying at his side. "I will fetch your brother."

Evie dipped into a hasty curtsy and then fled the chamber. She was not going to give up on him. But it was apparent that she needed to form a battle plan.

Chapter Fourteen

WHEN THEO WOKE again, it was to find Dom keeping vigil at his bedside. But the scent lingering on the air was undeniable, mixed with the medicinal tang of the sickroom. Warm, ripe fruit.

Evie, curse her beautiful, maddening, wonderful hide.

"Where is she?" he demanded, his voice nothing more than a rusty croak. As weak as his body felt.

"Who?" Dom asked as if he did not already know the answer.

There had never been another woman who had moved him, who affected him, the way Lady Evangeline Saltisford did. Pity she was a lady, betrothed to another man, and could never be his.

"Lady Evie," he bit out, his tongue feeling rough, too large. Dry. "Water?"

"Of course." Dom rose, crossed the room to a table where all manner of vials and tinctures and salves had been laid out, and poured water into a cup.

Devil supposed it was the same place Evie had fetched the water, but he had been a reckless knot of confusion, anger, good intentions, and feverish stupidity then. He had been furious to find her defying him, hating that she was once more where he wanted her, and yet he could not truly have her. Mind dulled by fever and sickness. When she had fled the room, he had fallen asleep once more, claimed by more nightmares.

This time, the flames had not engulfed him. The fevers attacking him seemed to have waned and thank Christ for that. He had been close to death, and he knew it.

Dom returned and held the cup to Devil's lips.

He drank greedily but slowly.

"Where is she?" he asked again after he had swallowed all he could manage and his voice was less than a reedy rumble at last.

"You were terrible to her," his brother observed instead of answering Devil's query. "A vicious arse."

He had been. Devil did not deny it.

"She will leave me anyway," he said instead of answering to what he had done. "May as well do it now."

He hated the notion of causing Evie pain. Everything he did was to make certain she was safe and happy. Even if her happiness was with another man, though the knowledge nearly flayed him alive.

"The lady seems to believe otherwise," his brother said calmly.

Of course she would. A duke's daughter knew nothing of hardship. A fortnight alone with him, and she fancied him what she wanted. A mere sennight in the rookeries, and she would change her mind, he had no doubt.

He did not possess an impressive house in the right part of town the way Dom did. He was not a gentleman, with a fancy cove's airs. He was not charming or smart. He answered adversity with his fists. He was a danger to her. His world was too dark, too grim, and there was no place for her light within it.

"Why have you allowed her to remain here?" Devil demanded, irritated anew.

"She is family," his brother said simply.

"To you. Not me." He scowled, the action making his already aching head hurt more. "I don't want her here."

"So you said, in quite cruel fashion, I understand."

"Because she is a lady and I am the bastard son of a ruthless merchant and a Covent Garden whore, neither of whom gave a damn about me," he said. "And I have nothing to offer her."

It was the bitter truth.

Undeniable.

"We are what we make of ourselves," his brother said. "You know that. You are a fine man. Lady Evie sees that. She cares for you."

Christ, how he wanted to believe that. The weakest part of him wanted to seize upon it with both hands. But the realistic part of him knew only one of his hands was currently in working order.

"She can't know that after a fortnight." He frowned at Dom.

Falling in love with Lady Adele had turned his brother into a dreamer.

"How can you make that decision for her, brother?" Dom returned.

Because he *had* to, but Devil did not say that aloud. One of them had to be the voice of reason. He could not bear to watch her leave him. And so, he would thrust her away. Then, her inevitable defection would not hurt so goddamned much. A clean break, now, was what they both needed.

"This world isn't for the likes of her," he told Dom. "I'll not have her resenting me, or growing to hate me for who I am the way Cora did."

He could still recall that long-ago day when she had left him.

When she had chosen to be a mistress instead of his wife.

The pain was old, the wound long healed into a scar. But the lesson remained. Cora had claimed to love him once. Evie had not suggested such tender feelings. If anything, she seemed to view him as an object of pity.

"If you think Cora and Lady Evangeline are anything alike, you've nothing but air betwixt those big ears of yours," Dom snapped, shaking Devil from his thoughts.

"I know her sort," he said simply. "I don't want her here."

"Then you must tell her that for yourself."

That was the problem, was it not? Or one of many, so it seemed. "I already have, and yet she remains."

Dom quirked a brow. "Mayhap you ought to think about that, brother."

Fuck.

He hated when Dom was right.

He glared at his half brother. "Mayhap," he allowed grudgingly, too tired to argue the point any further.

"You love her," Dom guessed.

Accurately, damn it. Devil did not know when he had realized the warmth inside his chest whenever she was near was love. That the fierce need to protect her from everyone and everything—including himself—had emerged because she owned his heart.

What a stupid twat he was. A hypocrite, believing Evie could not possibly know what she wanted after only a fortnight when that was all the time it had required for him to realize she was everything he had ever wanted but never dared to hope could be his.

She still couldn't.

Or could she?

"Devil?" Dom prodded, intruding on his madly whirling thoughts.

"I do," he admitted, a sense of finality washing over him, along with something else. It was tranquil and bright, like the sun after a vicious storm. "Bring her to me."

"HE HAS ASKED to see you."

Thank God.

Evie's heart leapt. She instantly quashed the elation. Joy and hope had no place until she heard Theo telling her he loved her.

Too much to hope at this juncture, she knew.

"How is he?" she asked her brother-in-law, desperate to know.

Hours had passed since this morning, when Theo had come to. She had kept her distance in deference to his wishes for the time being, but every moment she had spent waiting for word on his convalescence had been pure torture.

"He is on the mend, I believe," Dom told her, his expression pensive. "But there are some things I wish to tell you, Evie, so you can understand Devil a bit better."

"Yes." She nodded, eager for anything her brother-in-law would share. The Winters were quite protective of each other. She had noticed that already. Their bond was unbreakable.

Commendable, as well.

Forged of iron and love and pure determination.

"Devil and I…" Dom began and then paused, inhaling slowly, before exhaling. "Forgive me. It is a painful tale. We shared a father, it is true, but our mothers were not the same. When they discovered we shared the same sire, they decided to sell us both as brothers. They could fetch more for us that way. We were sold to an unscrupulous scoundrel who intended to use us in all manner of evil. We escaped thanks to

Devil. He saved me, and from that day forward, I have owed him…"

"That is why you are telling me all this now," Evie guessed.

"Aye," Dom agreed. "And also because I love my brother, and I can see quite plainly that you love him too. I want him to have the happiness I have found with your sister, the happiness he deserves. But there is also another painful part of his past, one which I doubt he has shared with you either."

Evie stiffened. "Another lady?"

Her brother-in-law nodded. "He fancied himself in love with her. It was a long time ago, and he was scarcely more than a lad. But she left him because she did not want to live this life, and instead she went on to become some fancy nib's mistress."

"I see."

Good heavens, she had never imagined there was a woman in Theo's past whom he had loved. She did not know what to do with this information. Indeed, she wished she had never had it foisted upon her.

"All I meant to say was that he has been hurt before by the women who should have loved him most, by those closest to him," Dom said then. "If he is…reluctant and gruff and cruel, it is not because he does not care. He does care for you. A great deal, I would wager."

She would prefer to hear all that from Theo himself.

But for now, she supposed it would have to be enough hearing them from his brother. "Thank you for sharing those bits of his past with me."

"I know you care for him, Evie," Dom said solemnly. "And I know he is an arse. But he is a good man. Give him a chance."

She smiled then. "I know he is a good man. And that is

why I have fallen in love with him." Evie paused, her smile widening wryly at the expression on her brother-in-law's face. "And no, I have not informed him yet. I am awaiting the right time."

"Trust me, my lady," Dom said, "there is no right time to be had. Just tell him. Those are the words he needs to hear more than any others."

Evie nodded. "I shall." She dipped into a perfunctory curtsy. "If you will excuse me?"

Dom bowed. Their stares met and held.

She had seen how much he was in love with her twin, and she had also come to respect him a great deal. She appreciated his guidance in this matter. And if it led to her winning Theo, then she was all the more thankful.

She hastened off in the direction of Theo's chamber without exchanging another word. Over the last two days, she had become so familiar with the inner layout of the private quarters of The Devil's Spawn that she could have lived there from birth. The rooms were surprisingly spacious, on a level above the gaming and club floors, quite secluded.

When she reached Theo's door, she knocked hesitantly. Once, then twice. No answer. She knocked harder.

At long last, his low, beloved baritone answered from within. "Come."

With a trembling hand, she let herself into his private domain. Unlike the countless other times she had crossed the threshold into his territory, this time was different. He was not out of his mind with fever or desperately ill. Instead, he was recovering.

"Milady."

His voice was not particularly welcoming. Nor was his expression.

She went inside anyway. "You called me Evie not so long

ago."

"You are still here," he said instead of responding to her prod.

"Yes." She seated herself primly at his side, every part of her longing to throw herself into his arms.

Gently, of course.

Her hungry gaze traveled over him. His color was already much improved. He looked…alive, vibrant. And handsome, in spite of the fading bruises and gauntness of his face.

"Why?"

"Because I belong here." She reached for his right hand, settling hers gently atop it. "I belong where you are."

"You belong in Mayfair," he growled.

"No." She took a deep breath, summoning her daring. "I belong with the man I love."

He stilled, his expression changing at last. Softening. "Evie."

"I love you, Theo." Telling him felt right. She should have done so before now, but fear had kept her from making the revelation.

She would not allow it to stop her this time.

"You are not meant for this life," he said quietly.

Not the words of love she had been hoping for.

"I am meant for a life with you," she countered.

He closed his eyes, his countenance turning pained. "Do not say something you will later regret."

She laced her fingers through his, gratified he had not withdrawn from her touch. "I will never regret telling you I love you and belong at your side. Stop pushing me away. Let me into your heart."

"Fucking hell."

His bitter oath told her he was fighting a losing battle.

"Please, Theo," she said.

His eyes opened, vivid blue burning into her. "You are the daughter of a duke."

"I am the woman who loves you," she countered. "That is what matters most."

"Damn it, Evie." He glared at her, rolling his lips inward as if he were attempting to suppress words.

She brought his hand to her lips, pressing a kiss to it, then to the inking of the blade on his inner wrist. "You can say the words."

He grunted.

But his stern demeanor was fading. She kissed his hand again, holding his gaze. "Theo?"

"I love you, too," he admitted on a rush.

Her heart suddenly felt too big for her body. "You do?"

He glowered. "Aye. I do."

Relief and joy—profound, deep, overwhelming, blossomed. He *loved* her.

"You do not still want to send me away?" she pressed.

"I'll not have you regret this decision," he said. "I want you to be sure."

"I am sure." She shook her head, smiling at him through a sudden rush of tears. "I have never been surer of anything or anyone."

His gaze searched hers. "What of Dullerton?"

She knew a brief pang of guilt at the manner in which she had defected. Mayhap there would be scandal. Her reputation could be ruined if she married Theo. She did not care. Lord Denton could find solace in the arms of Mrs. Hale.

She squeezed Theo's fingers. "I wrote him a letter. I've cried off. There is only one man I want to marry."

He brought their entwined hands to his lips for a reverent kiss. "It had damn well better be me."

"Then you had better ask me, Mr. Theodore Winter," she

countered lightly, trying to keep her tears of happiness at bay.

"Lady Evangeline Saltisford," he said formally, kissing each one of her fingers, then her upturned palm.

She swallowed. "Yes?"

"Marry me?"

All the hope and love and elation burst open inside her, like a tightly furled bud blossoming in the sun. "I thought you would never ask."

He tugged her. "Come here."

She crawled on the bed, nestling beside him, taking care not to jostle him too much. He curved his good arm around her, holding her to his side as he dropped a kiss on the top of her head. She embraced him, resting her palm over the promising thud of his heart.

"Was that a yes?" he asked.

She tipped her head back, smiling into his brilliant eyes. "Of course it was."

Chapter Fifteen

DEVIL WAS NOT certain which three words he preferred more, *Mrs. Theodore Winter* or *I love you.*

Looking at the woman who had just become his wife, he decided he didn't need to choose. They were all excellent. Perfect, in fact. As perfect as she was, dressed in a night rail that had surely been crafted to make him fall to his knees with crazed lust.

It was successful.

His knees wanted to buckle, just looking at her.

"My God, Evie."

She cast him a shy smile. Her golden curls were unbound, cascading over her shoulders. Her nipples were hard temptations prodding the fine fabric of her gown. The sight of her standing there in her chamber at the townhome he had managed to secure next door to Dom and Lady Adele's stole his breath. They had waited months to marry, and the delay had been excruciating.

But he had been determined to win her father's approval and to heal and regain the use of his arm. He had also set about creating a life for himself beyond The Devil's Spawn. A life that would be worthy of his wife. None of it had been easy. But he had done it, damn it. For Evie.

"Shall I wrap a counterpane about me like a shawl?" she teased him.

Reminding him of that long-ago night when he had been desperately tempted to take her. But that had been before she was his.

She was his now.

"No counterpane needed tonight, love," he answered, stopping before her and running his knuckle down her jaw.

Her skin was softer than silk. Her scent twined itself around him. Her brown-gold eyes shimmered up at him with love. He could not stop touching her. He trailed his fingers down her throat next.

She swallowed. "Theo?"

He buried his face in her neck, inhaling deeply. "Yes?"

"I love you."

He would never grow tired of hearing that. Or of touching her. Her warmth burned him through the banyan he had donned. He pressed nearer to her, seeking the connection of their bodies. Her curves melted into his hard frame. He kissed her pounding pulse.

"And I love you." He kissed his way to her ear, nibbling on the shell.

She shivered. He had missed her responsiveness. Had missed everything about being alone with her. Her skin, her scent, her lips. Licking her until she came on his tongue.

"The last few months of playing the gentleman were fucking awful," he grumbled, and then he could not prolong the torture any longer. He took her lips with his.

She made a sound of surrender, sighing and clutching his shoulders as her lips moved against his, opening. He slid his tongue inside her mouth, and she sucked on it, as if she were ravenous for him. He groaned, deepening the kiss, his fingers trailing over every expanse of her luscious body they could find. He wanted to touch her everywhere, to imprint the memory of her curves upon his fingertips. He wanted to lick her and taste her and kiss her. To fuck her and fill her.

He caressed her waist, took handfuls of her rump and ground her against his cock, allowing her to feel how much he wanted her. No more gentleman tonight. Heat flared up his spine. He was a starving man, and she was his feast.

He moved them, kissing her as he went, intending to guide them to the bed. In the newness of his surroundings and the daze of his passion, he missed the mark. He realized his error too late when Evie's back collided with the wall.

Too damn bad. He would just have her here first. He broke the kiss, taking a moment to gaze down at her, to drink in the sight of her. He ran his hands through her tresses, lightly tugging at the ends so she allowed her head to fall against the wall, revealing more of her neck to him.

He kissed and sucked, rasping the prickle of his whiskers—freshly shaven that morning and already returning—over her delicate skin. He was ferocious now. His fingers left her hair to work on the row of buttons on the bodice of her night gown. But there were too many of the bloody things, and he lost his patience.

He took his mouth off her long enough to grasp handfuls of the fabric and pull it over her head. "You've gotten more beautiful in the months we've waited."

He drank in the sight of her. The flare of her hips, her luscious thighs, full, high breasts tipped with jutting pink nipples. Devil sucked the peak of one into his mouth. She arched her back, thrusting her breasts forward, the breathy moan emerging from her telling him everything he needed to know. He cupped her other breast, thumb working over her nipple.

And then he could not resist dropping to his knees. He hooked her leg over his shoulder and licked her. She was soaked, the scent of her need perfuming the air in a way that made his cock twitch.

"So perfect," he murmured against her folds. "You have the prettiest cunny."

Her fingers tunneled through his hair. He liked the dance of them on his scalp, the way her nails gently raked over him. He sank his tongue inside her, filling her the way he would soon with another part of him. *God*, she tasted good. Like summer. Like her.

Like *his*.

He thrust into her again and again before turning his attention to the pouting bud of her pearl. He sucked hard, then nipped, slipping a finger inside her channel at the same time. Her panting breaths were music. He was attuned to her, becoming one with her, and despite the pulsing in his ballocks, he thought he could stay like this forever, pinning her to the wall, making love to her until she could no longer stand. She tightened on his finger, and he worked her harder. Merciless, relentless, alternating between sucks and licks until she cried out, her body stiffening, her cunny clamping on his finger.

He withdrew from her and rose to his feet, blood roaring through him. Her eyes were wide, her lips parted. Devil traced over their lush fullness, painting her lips with her own dew and then sliding the fleshy pad into her mouth.

"See how sweet you taste," he told her.

She sucked, and he thought his head might explode.

He removed the digit and replaced it with his mouth, kissing her frantically, feverishly. The taste of her mingled on their lips and tongues. It was hot, wet, feral. She moaned into the kiss. His fingers found their way between her thighs, dipping past her soaked curls to tease her nub once more.

She writhed against him, pressing her hard nipples into his chest, reminding him he was still wearing a banyan. To hell with this barrier between them. He wanted to be naked now. Wanted his skin on Evie's at last. Wanted her to sear him from head to toe. Devil clawed at the belt, shucked his robe.

Breaking the kiss, he took her in his arms.

A twinge of pain went through his healed shoulder, but it was worth it to hold her like this again. Not long ago, he had been unsure of whether or not he ever could again.

"Theo!" She was breathless, arms flying around his neck for purchase. "You will hurt yourself."

"You're light as a bird, love," he assured her, stalking with her to the bed.

He had worked hard to regain his strength after he had been wounded. Fortunately, he had the constitution of a mule.

"Theo," she protested again.

"Hush, Mrs. Winter." He dropped a kiss on her lips, then placed her on the bed with gentle care. "I worked hard for this moment, and I intend to enjoy it—and you—to the hilt."

He settled between her legs on the bed, starting where he had left off, his fingers parting her slick folds. He licked her nipple, leveraged himself on his left forearm, pleased when the lingering pain was eclipsed by desire. She was wet, so wet. And hot. Her body undulated against him, seeking more, urging him on with her hips.

Devil sucked the peak of her other breast, then grazed it with his teeth.

"Oh," she said.

She liked him a little rough, his Evie. Good, because he was wild for her. And the hold he had on his restraint was growing slippery. He suckled her and played with her and she came beautifully, body bowing from the bed. She was so wet by now that the sound of his fingers sliding through her folds echoed in the chamber.

He had to be inside her.

Soon.

But Evie had other intentions, it seemed. In the aftermath of her second crisis, she flattened her palms on his shoulders, guiding him to his back. He did as she wanted, lying there with awareness humming through him. The sheets were cool and soft on his back. His cock was hard, ballocks drawn tight with need. She straddled him, those creamy thighs on either side of his hips.

Good God, he had a perfect view of the tempting folds of her sex, parting. Of the swollen pearl peeking from her curls. His mouth watered for another taste of her. The sinner in him wondered if he could convince her to sit on his face so he could thrust his tongue deep inside her until she came again.

But then he forced himself to remember she was a virgin. Although they had made good use of their fleeting moments alone over the past few months, he had refused to bed her until she was his wife. He reached for her breasts, weighing them in his palms. They were perfect handfuls.

"I want to worship you," she told him shyly.

He felt like an ungainly, massive creature trapped beneath a goddess. He was aware of his scars, his every mark of ink. On his chest, on his upper arm, the puckered, pink flesh from the most recent bullet.

"I am nothing to worship," he rasped.

She shook her head, a beautiful smile curving her lips. "How wrong you are, Theodore Winter. You are perfect."

"Flawed."

She dipped her head and pressed a kiss to his healed wound. "Perfect."

Ah, fuck. Tenderness warred with desire.

"A beast," he ground out. "Covered in ink and scars."

"*My* beast." She kissed across his chest, her mouth anointing every mark, every wound, all the pieces of his past. "I love your scars. I love your ink." Those tormenting lips traveled to his throat. "I love *you*."

He was damned glad she did, because he loved her too. More every day. More than he thought possible.

She kissed his other shoulder, then made her way to his jaw, kissing to his lips with slow, maddening precision. Devil could not wait another moment. He caught her chin and angled her head, sealing their mouths. They kissed long and deep, an exchange of emotion too profound for mere words.

Then she broke the kiss and changed her position, settling between his legs on her knees as she kissed down his chest, following the thin trail of dark hair that led directly to his straining cockstand.

"Evie," he ground out, not wanting her to take him in her mouth. And also desperately wanting her to take him in her mouth.

She kissed the tip, and when her tongue flicked out to taste him, he could not suppress a moan. Damn, but it was glorious. Until she licked a circle around him before sucking his cock into her pretty mouth. And then it was more than glorious. Wet heat engulfed him. He was in heaven. Bliss. He had died and this was Elysium. He never wanted it to end.

He could not keep still. His hips pumped, sending him deeper into her mouth.

Fuck. If it didn't end soon, he was going to spill before he was inside her.

Devil reached for her, hauling her up his body before rolling her onto her back once again.

EVIE WAS ON her back, Theo a welcome, muscular weight wedged between her thighs. His mouth was on hers, feasting, feeding. Love and desire swirled through her, making her almost dizzied with the force of it. She trembled beneath his questing hands, beneath his supple lips and fierce kisses.

All the months they had waited to be married had been worth it for this.

For him.

She would have waited forever, if she'd had to. Evie was quite glad she hadn't had to.

She held Theo to her, wrapping her legs around his hips. His familiar, beloved scent washed over her. Leather, bay, man. *Theo.* Her fingertips trailed over his broad shoulders, seeking anywhere she could touch him. His manhood was rigid and thick and tempting, prodding her throbbing flesh where she wanted him most.

It was almost impossible to believe he was hers at last.

That they were married, the promise of their life together before them, bright as the morning sun. She was still the daughter of a duke, but now she was Mrs. Theodore Winter, and that was the title she wore with the most pride. Their tongues tangled. Heat pooled between her thighs. She ached for him to touch her there.

His lips moved, enchanting her everywhere they traveled. He dropped kisses all over her without pattern or reason. Collarbone, shoulder, nipple. The inside of her elbow. Her hip. Lower, to her knee. Her ankle. He kissed the arch of her foot, his gaze hot and dark-blue, arresting in its intensity. He kissed her in places she had never dreamt she would long to be kissed. But this was Theo, and everywhere his lips found her, the fires of passion raged. She writhed on the bed, desperate for more.

The flames roared higher.

His lips moved along her inner thigh, nearing her center.

She ached.

"I want inside you, Evie," he whispered against her skin. "I want inside you so badly."

"Yes." She wanted that too. She wanted him desperately. Anything. Everything.

She was panting with her need, breathless, heart pounding.

"I don't want to hurt you, love." He kissed her mound, and she jerked beneath him, quite shameless. "I am big and you are so bloody small."

"You shan't hurt me," she promised him, for she knew it was the truth.

He was Theo, kind and sweet. A tender heart wrapped in a big, lumbering body. He would be gentle. For a man who had been the recipient of such cold cruelty in his life—for he had confessed to her, over the last few months, all of his past, from his mother to Cora, to the hard life he had led for so long—he was astonishingly sweet.

"I need to make you ready," he whispered, licking over the incredibly sensitized bundle of flesh he had already pleasured numerous times.

"I am ready," she assured him, and would have said more if he hadn't nibbled on her, sending white-hot desire shooting through her like stars. She jolted beneath him, moaning, shamelessly planting her feet on the bed to drive herself higher, to offer more of herself to him.

Good heavens. If this was what he wanted to do, she could most certainly become *more* ready. One of his long fingers was inside her again, probing. He sucked as his finger moved deeper, stretching her. The invasion was delicious. A second finger joined the first, stroking her, readying her. All the while, his tongue danced over her. Making her wild.

She grasped his hair. Two fistfuls, and tugged. "Now, Theo."

He met her gaze and sucked hard, working his fingers in and out. The pleasure was almost painful. A curious mix. Foreign. She needed more. More him. More everything. And she was perilously close to coming undone again.

Just when she thought she would perish from the endless pleasure he stoked within her, he withdrew his fingers and kissed his way up her body. He lingered on her breasts, sucking and gently biting her nipples as he rubbed the thickness of his rod over her folds.

When the tip of him rubbed over her pearl, she moaned, her hips moving, seeking more. She was wet, so wet, between her thighs, her flesh swollen and throbbing. He kissed to her throat, then her ear. He slid along her folds, settling at her opening.

Yes. This was where she wanted him. Where she needed him.

"Inside me," she ordered him on a gasp.

"What milady wants, milady gets," he whispered into her ear, before catching her lobe between his teeth and giving her a gentle bite.

She shivered and trembled, eagerness making her mindless. He licked the hollow behind her ear, finding yet another place she had never known was sensitive. It was as if there were a hidden connection between that place and her sex.

"Oh," she said on a moan.

Theo kissed her cheek next, then her jaw. He moved. The change was sudden and intense. He was indeed a big man. Every part of him was large. Especially this part. And she was small. His hips pumped, taking him deeper. He was inside her now, stretching her, filling her, and the sensation of it was unlike his fingers, unlike his tongue. It was...beautiful.

He held himself still, allowing her to adjust, his chest pressed to hers. His heart was pounding. She absorbed the beats through her breast. He kissed her slowly, lingeringly, cupping her cheek.

As if she were made of porcelain.

"Darling," he said against her lips. "Christ, you feel so good. I am afraid I may lose control."

"I want you to." She kissed him, locking her arms around his neck as she rocked against him, bringing him deeper.

He thrust again on a groan as his tongue slid wetly into her mouth. She sucked, and he thrust some more.

Pain edged the pleasure. It was new. Strange. Exhilarating. She felt as if she might break apart into a thousand pieces at any moment. And she also felt as if she would never get enough. He moved in and out of her, and she could feel her body reacting to his. She surrounded him, and he sank into her. They were united and joined in a way they had never been before.

"Yes," she told him, her body moving instinctively along with his.

The tension building within her threatened to explode.

She was burning, awash in sensation. Nothing could have prepared her for this, Theo's lovemaking. It was him—loving and intense, sweet and delicious. He started moving faster, driving his hips against hers in a steady rhythm. Withdrawing, then sliding inside again. Faster. Harder.

She followed his lead, moving with him. Their lips and tongues mated, their bodies connected. His fingers dipped to the place where they were joined, toying with her pearl once more. The pain receded, replaced by nothing but pleasure, acute and beautiful. She was going to come undone. Lose herself again. There was something about the fullness inside her, of Theo plunging deep, that was almost unbearably pleasurable.

He left her mouth to rain kisses on her throat, chanting her name, thrusting. Everything within tightened, as if drawn into a knot. Bliss exploded inside her, rocking her to her core. It was stronger, better, more powerful. She quaked beneath him, surrendering herself to the undeniable passion.

On a growl, he began moving faster, taking her in a series of quick, hard thrusts that had her clamping on him again, lighting her from within. He stiffened, pinned her to the bed with one last thrust, and then the warmth of his seed flooded her.

He collapsed against her, his weight nearly crushing, his heart beating faster than ever. Her sweet beast, tamed at last. She held him to her, kissing the top of his head, then rubbing her cheek over his thick, dark hair.

"Evie. Sweet fuck." He was breathless.

She smiled and stroked his back, holding him to her when he would have retreated. "Sweet fuck indeed."

"Hell." He raised his head, gazing down at her with a look of such undisguised adoration, she melted inside. "You ought not repeat me, love. I've a wicked tongue."

Her smile grew. "I know you do, and I love it."

He chuckled. "Minx."

"Your minx," she reminded him, her heart full.

"Mine," he agreed, and then he kissed her again.

Epilogue

"*FOR NEVER WAS a story of more woe than this of Juliet and her Romeo*," Devil finished, his throat feeling thick and his eyes strangely watery.

He was a hesitant reader, and he still stumbled over many words, but he had vastly improved with Evie's patience and help. It had been her idea to finish *Romeo and Juliet* together, with Devil reading.

A decision he regretted now.

Well fuck me, that's a bloody sad ending. He had seen it coming, of course, but he had been hopeful all would end differently. That Juliet and her Romeo might find a way to be together and happy after all, just as he had with Evie.

He glanced up from the volume he had been reading to find his wife watching him with a strange expression. He wanted to kiss her. She was wearing the night rail that was temptingly transparent, but it was stretched over her burgeoning belly, where their child grew. Soon, she would have to have another commissioned, and then she could tempt him with that one instead. He hardened just thinking about it—the forthcoming removal of this one, and what the next one might look like.

There. That was much more the thing.

Her nose crinkled. "Are you…weeping?"

Impossible. Devil Winter did not nap the bib. He never

cried. He had not wept a single tear since he had been a lad. Even then, it had not taken him long to understand the fruitlessness of such an endeavor. The woman who had birthed him had cuffed him for his troubles. He was to be seen, not heard, and if he wasn't picking pockets to pay for the bread on the table, he was worthless to her.

But his cheeks were wet. He realized it belatedly. No denying that. The play was terrifically sad. What was a man to do?

"It is tragic," he admitted. "Senseless. The two of them should have been happy."

"Oh, my love." There was tremendous tenderness in her voice, in her gaze. "You have such a sweet heart."

Maudlin sentiment.

He growled. "I have something else that is sweeter if you'd care for a taste."

Her cheeks flushed the pretty pink he loved, but her smile was secretive and seductive all at once. "If you wish it..."

He groaned. His cock was painfully rigid at the moment.

"Not now, love. I was attempting to distract you." He sniffed, trying to discreetly wipe his eyes with the back of his hand and failing. His big, meaty paws were anything but subtle. "To make you laugh. Didn't want you to think I've gone soft because I got a wee bit teary-eyed over Montague and Capulet."

"I could never think you are soft," she said, her stare dipping to his breeches.

Damn, but his wife would never cease to amaze and please him.

"Mrs. Winter, I am shocked," he teased warmly.

"Forgive me, Mr. Winter." She batted her lashes and rose, strolling toward him. She took the book from his hands and then settled herself in his lap. "How can I regain your favor?"

He had a few ideas. More than a few, actually.

He kissed her swiftly on that delicious pout of hers, then withdrew. "I can think of any number of ways."

"Mmm." She pulled him back down for another lingering kiss, which she ended abruptly, tearing her lips from his. "Oh dear. I meant to tell you that I wrote Lady Emilia today with my regrets, telling her we shan't be able to attend your brother's Christmas country house party at Abingdon Hall."

Perdition. This was not a change of subject that pleased him. It still felt deuced strange thinking of Devereaux Winter as his family.

"Half brother," he reminded her, stroking a stray curl from her face.

"It was quite kind of your brother and Lady Emilia to invite us," she continued, ignoring his correction. "Do you suppose they will be insulted we cannot attend?"

"I don't care if he is. You'd have to be spoony to go to Oxfordshire for a house party in the midst of winter. Or at any time, really." Devil still didn't care for the monkery. Not one whit.

"Blade will be in attendance," Evie pointed out.

Devil settled his hand on the gentle swell of his wife's belly. "Because he had no choice. Dom banished him. Also, he's spoony. Have you ever seen him play with knives?"

He loved Blade as he loved all his siblings, but Devil was no more pleased than Dom had been by their brother's recent reckless actions. He had brought scandal down upon The Devil's Spawn at a time when they could least afford it. Along with the potential for more danger.

"I still think it was harsh of Dom to send him away." Evie covered his hand with hers, lacing their fingers together.

"The monkery is an excellent place for him. Not much trouble he can get into there. Besides, the rest of my siblings will be joining him, aside from Dom." Devil tugged her mouth back to his with his free hand. Winter swirled outside, blanketing the streets of London in early snow. But he was on fire for Evie, and he'd had enough chatter. "Seems we have some lessons to attend to, milady. I've taught you the art of whittling, you've taught me the art of reading. But the time has come for us to teach each other the art of—"

She kissed him, silencing the rest of his words.

Which was just as well. It would have been quite crude. One could remove the man from the rookeries, but one could never remove the rookeries from the man. Good thing his sweet lady wife did not mind, duke's daughter and all.

THE END.

Dear Reader,

Thank you for reading *Winter's Woman*! I hope you loved this ninth book in my *The Wicked Winters* series and that Evie and Devil's happily ever after touched your heart the way it did mine. As always, thank you for spending your precious time reading my books!

Please consider leaving an honest review of *Winter's Woman*. Reviews are greatly appreciated! If you'd like to keep up to date with my latest releases and series news, sign up for my newsletter (scarlettscottauthor.com/contact) or follow me on Amazon or BookBub. Join my reader's group on Facebook for bonus content, early excerpts, giveaways, and more.

There are more Winters on the way. If you'd like a preview of *Winter's Whispers*, Book Ten in *The Wicked Winters* series, featuring dangerously debonair Blade Winter and the lady who steals his heart, do read on.

Until next time,

Scarlett

Winter's Whispers

The Wicked Winters Book Ten

By
Scarlett Scott

Don't miss this special addition to the bestselling The Wicked Winters series, featuring Winter family favorites and a whole lot of holiday steam!

Blade Winter is a coldhearted assassin with a deadly reputation. After a costly mistake leaves him banished to the countryside for a Christmas house party he has no wish to attend, he is furious. No amount of merrymaking is going to improve his mood. Until he crosses paths with a beautiful brunette he can never have, and suddenly, the prospect of a yuletide rusticating in Oxfordshire is not nearly as detestable…

Lady Felicity Hughes may be London's darling, but she is hiding a desperate secret. No one knows she must wed to save her family from penury, and she intends to keep it that way. But before she binds herself in a loveless marriage of convenience, she wants one night of passion. Who better to have it with than the wickedly handsome Mr. Winter?

Blade knows better than to dally with a lady who is forbidden, no matter how much she tempts him. Felicity is equally determined to get what she wants, even if there can be no future between herself and a dangerous man like Blade. She has nothing left to lose. Except her heart.

Chapter One

Oxfordshire, 1814

THERE WAS A female beneath his bed.

Trouble, warned his instincts.

A female was what had landed Blade here, in the monkery, at a cursed country house party being held by his half brother Devereaux Winter.

Not this particular one, though. He would have recognized the ankles. Blade was a connoisseur of ankles. And knives. Not necessarily in that order.

This one's ankles were fine boned, nicely turned, covered in pale stockings. He noted those first. He noted her arse second. A plummy handful, that. Too bad it was draped in an unappealing gown of virginal white. Virgins weren't his sort.

Innocence wasn't his sort.

Blade preferred debauched. Sinful widows, wicked wives. A woman who wasn't afraid to suck a cock.

Which was why the miss rooting about beneath his bed needed to go. At once.

He cleared his throat, hoping the strange bit of petticoats would realize she was no longer alone. But she did not emerge. Instead, she wriggled about, emphasizing the tempting qualities of her ankles and rump. *Damn.* Too bloody bad he was here to stay out of trouble. Those ankles presented a strong temptation to create an exception to his rule.

There was a muffled sound emerging from beneath the bed now. He closed the door at his back and strode nearer, drawn by a combination of perplexity and attraction. *By God*, was the woman having a conversation? Beneath his bed?

"Miss Wilhelmina, do come," the strange creature was saying in a sweet, cajoling voice that would have certainly worked wonders upon Blade. She had the voice of an angel, this one. "I shall give you liver, I promise."

The devil?

Blade crouched down by the shapely bottom, curiosity triumphing over patience. "What the hell is under my bed?"

"Ahhhh!"

Her scream was muffled, but the jolt that went through her body was evident, as was the undeniable sound of her head connecting with the wooden slats on the underside of the bed.

She muttered something that sounded suspiciously like an epithet.

If he were a gentleman, he would cease ogling her arse, but he wasn't, so he kept watching as she wiggled, slowly emerging from beneath the bed. He had never been much concerned about a woman's derriere, but there was something about this one that was mesmerizing. He imagined cupping it in his hands, shaping and molding it.

Not now, Blade, you bloody sot. It is not the time to get a cockstand when there is an innocent miss hiding beneath the bed along with a creature she has promised liver.

As she sidled her way from beneath the bed, he could not help also admiring the manner in which her gown and petticoats were bunching up as she went, revealing more and more of her curved, stocking-clad legs. She was deliciously shapely, but that was not something he ought to be noticing either.

The duel he had fought with the Earl of Penhurst had

been enough for his half brother Dom to banish him from London and their gaming hell, The Devil's Spawn. Petticoats were dangerous, and he did not need any more problems than those which currently bogged him down.

Still, it did not help when the creamy skin of her thighs, just above her stockings, was exposed. Nor did it do a whit of good when she finally emerged, a dark-haired beauty with wide, hazel eyes and the most inviting pair of pink lips he had ever seen. To say nothing of her bosom, spilling over the top of her modest gown. Apparently, her foray beneath his bed had also rendered her bodice askew. Her cheeks were prettily flushed. Everything about the woman who had slithered from beneath his bed was delectable.

This was going to be a problem. He could bloody well sense it.

"Sir!" She rubbed her head. "It was terribly rude of you, speaking without announcing yourself. I may have done myself great injury."

Incredible.

The baggage was taking him to task. She was a lady, that much he could spy instantly. Her gown was fine, though not as bang up to the mark as Lady Penhurst's fashion. Her voice was cool, clipped.

Aristocratic.

He passed his hand along his jaw, allowing his gaze to roam over her freely. "Reckon the rude one is the one who stuffed herself beneath my bed."

Her flush deepened, creeping down her throat. "I am attempting to rescue Miss Wilhelmina."

"Miss Wilhelmina," he repeated.

Mayhap her wits were addled. He had yet to see a sign of anything under the bed save her.

"My kitten." She struggled with her gown, belatedly

covering her limbs.

A feline. He was appalled. Cats were detestable animals. The offer of liver finally made sense.

"Christ." His lip curled. "Get it out of here."

She frowned at him. "That is what I was trying to do when you interrupted me, sir."

"Blade," he corrected, sketching a mocking bow. "No sir. No mister."

Her frown deepened, that hazel gaze of hers—not quite green, nor brown, yet almost gray—searched his. "I beg your pardon?"

"The name's Blade Winter. Half brother to the host. Very reluctant guest. Ardent hater of cats," he listed off each fact idly, watching her, fascinated by her in spite of himself. "Definitely not the sort of cove you ought to find yourself alone with, in a bedchamber."

Her brows rose. The becoming pink flush had reached the tops of her breasts now. "Oh dear."

Bloody hell. Mayhap a fortnight trapped in the wintry wilds of England was not going to be nearly as boring as he had supposed.

Want more? Get *Winter's Whispers*!

Don't miss Scarlett's other romances!

(Listed by Series)

Complete Book List
scarlettscottauthor.com/books

HISTORICAL ROMANCE

Heart's Temptation
A Mad Passion (Book One)
Rebel Love (Book Two)
Reckless Need (Book Three)
Sweet Scandal (Book Four)
Restless Rake (Book Five)
Darling Duke (Book Six)
The Night Before Scandal (Book Seven)

Wicked Husbands
Her Errant Earl (Book One)
Her Lovestruck Lord (Book Two)
Her Reformed Rake (Book Three)
Her Deceptive Duke (Book Four)
Her Missing Marquess (Book Five)
Her Virtuous Viscount (Book Six)

League of Dukes
Nobody's Duke (Book One)
Heartless Duke (Book Two)
Dangerous Duke (Book Three)
Shameless Duke (Book Four)
Scandalous Duke (Book Five)

Fearless Duke (Book Six)

Notorious Ladies of London
Lady Ruthless (Book One)
Lady Wallflower (Book Two)
Lady Reckless (Book Three)
Lady Wicked (Book Four)

The Wicked Winters
Wicked in Winter (Book One)
Wedded in Winter (Book Two)
Wanton in Winter (Book Three)
Wishes in Winter (Book 3.5)
Willful in Winter (Book Four)
Wagered in Winter (Book Five)
Wild in Winter (Book Six)
Wooed in Winter (Book Seven)
Winter's Wallflower (Book Eight)
Winter's Woman (Book Nine)
Winter's Whispers (Book Ten)
Winter's Waltz (Book Eleven)

Stand-alone Novella
Lord of Pirates

CONTEMPORARY ROMANCE

Love's Second Chance
Reprieve (Book One)
Perfect Persuasion (Book Two)
Win My Love (Book Three)

Coastal Heat
Loved Up (Book One)

About the Author

USA Today and Amazon bestselling author Scarlett Scott writes steamy Victorian and Regency romance with strong, intelligent heroines and sexy alpha heroes. She lives in Pennsylvania with her Canadian husband, adorable identical twins, and one TV-loving dog.

A self-professed literary junkie and nerd, she loves reading anything, but especially romance novels, poetry, and Middle English verse. Catch up with her on her website www.scarlettscottauthor.com. Hearing from readers never fails to make her day.

Scarlett's complete book list and information about upcoming releases can be found at www.scarlettscottauthor.com.

Connect with Scarlett! You can find her here:
Join Scarlett Scott's reader's group on Facebook for early excerpts, giveaways, and a whole lot of fun!
Sign up for her newsletter here.
scarlettscottauthor.com/contact
Follow Scarlett on Amazon
Follow Scarlett on BookBub
www.instagram.com/scarlettscottauthor
www.twitter.com/scarscoromance
www.pinterest.com/scarlettscott
www.facebook.com/AuthorScarlettScott